PAINFUL GOOD-BYES

"I ain't taking no more orders from you, Slocum."

"All right," Slocum said. "Have it your way." He turned as if to walk away, then spun back around quickly, grabbing Pool's right wrist and holding it tight, while driving his own right hand deep into Pool's gut. Pool lost all of his wind and dropped the knife. Slocum brought up a knee, smashing Pool's face. Then he grabbed Pool's shirt and slung him to the ground. Julia quickly bent down to pick up the knife. She held it behind her back. Pool groaned and got to his knees. He wiped at the blood on his face with his sleeve.

"You broke my nose, you son of a bitch," he said. "You broke my fucking nose."

"Saddle up your horse and get out of here," Slocum said.

"You owe me money."

"Not anymore I don't. Saddle it up."

JAKE LOGAN

SLOCUM AND THE BOSS'S WIFE

JOVE BOOKS, NEW YORK

THE BERKLEY PUBLISHING GROUP
Published by the Penguin Group
Penguin Group (USA) Inc.
375 Hudson Street, New York, New York 10014, USA
Penguin Group (Canada), 90 Eglinton Avenue East, Suite 700, Toronto, Ontario M4P 2Y3, Canada
(a division of Pearson Penguin Canada Inc.)
Penguin Books Ltd., 80 Strand, London WC2R 0RL, England
Penguin Group Ireland, 25 St. Stephen's Green, Dublin 2, Ireland (a division of Penguin Books Ltd.)
Penguin Group (Australia), 250 Camberwell Road, Camberwell, Victoria 3124, Australia
(a division of Pearson Australia Group Pty. Ltd.)
Penguin Books India Pvt. Ltd., 11 Community Centre, Panchsheel Park, New Delhi—110 017, India
Penguin Group (NZ), Cnr. Airborne and Rosedale Roads, Albany, Auckland 1310, New Zealand
(a division of Pearson New Zealand Ltd.)
Penguin Books (South Africa) (Pty.) Ltd., 24 Sturdee Avenue, Rosebank, Johannesburg 2196,
South Africa

Penguin Books Ltd., Registered Offices: 80 Strand, London WC2R 0RL, England

This is a work of fiction. Names, characters, places, and incidents either are the product of the author's imagination or are used fictitiously, and any resemblance to actual persons, living or dead, business establishments, events, or locales is entirely coincidental.

SLOCUM AND THE BOSS'S WIFE

A Jove Book / published by arrangement with the author

PRINTING HISTORY
Jove edition / March 2006

Copyright © 2006 by The Berkley Publishing Group.

ISBN: 0-515-14090-2

JOVE®
Jove Books are published by The Berkley Publishing Group,
a division of Penguin Group (USA) Inc.
375 Hudson Street, New York, New York 10014.
JOVE is a registered trademark of Penguin Group (USA) Inc.
The "J" design is a trademark belonging to Penguin Group (USA) Inc.

PRINTED IN THE UNITED STATES OF AMERICA

10 9 8 7 6 5 4 3 2 1

1

Slocum had a job to do. It was a hell of a tough job, and so far, it had not been pleasant, but someone would do it if he did not, and the money was good. Asa Hodges, a big rancher with more money than sense, had hired Slocum for a simple cowhand's job at cowhand's wages, but he had called Slocum in one day to see him in the big house. Slocum found Hodges seated behind his big desk, reared back and looking pompous as hell. Hodges looked up when Slocum walked in.

"Slocum," he had said, "I've been watching you."

"I been doing my job," Slocum said.

"I know. But you're not an ordinary cowhand, are you?"

"Something you don't like about the way I work?"

"You're doing all right, Slocum, but I think you're a god damned gunslinger. Am I wrong about that?"

"I can handle myself when the need arises," Slocum said, "but if you're afraid of having me around, just say so. I'll draw what wages I got coming to me and hit the trail. It ain't nothing new to me."

"Now, don't go putting words into my mouth. Hear me out." Hodges opened a box on his desktop and took out a cigar. He stuck it in his mouth and motioned to the box. "Help yourself," he said. Slocum took one out. Hodges took a match from another box, and Slocum did the same. There was a pause in the conversation while the two men fired up their smokes. "Sit down, Slocum," Hodges said. Slocum parked his ass in the chair just across the big desk from his boss.

"You got something on your mind, Mr. Hodges?" Slocum said.

"My wife's been kidnapped," Hodges said.

Slocum was a bit surprised at the abruptness with which that information was put forth, but then, he had called for it.

"I know who did it," Hodges continued. "It was Daryl O'Neill. He runs the Big O spread over in the next county."

"You sure it was him?" Slocum asked.

"Damn sure. I've sent men over there after her, but none of them had any luck. I want you to bring her home. I'll pay you well. Ten thousand dollars. Just bring her home. That's all."

Slocum puffed at his cigar. It was a good one, expensive. "You make it sound real simple," he said. "What happened when them others rode after her?"

"O'Neill's men drove them off with guns," Hodges said. "One of my men was killed the last time. If it's not enough money—"

"It's enough for me," Slocum said, "but I won't take this job on all by my lonesome. I'll need some help. Good help."

"I'll give you another ten thousand, and you can use it any way you want. Stick it in your own pocket or hire more men with it. I don't care how you do it, I just want her brought home. It's up to you. What do you say?"

Slocum took the job. He also took another of Hodges's hands, a young cowboy named Gil Harman. Harman was bold, and he was handy with his guns. Slocum had seen him knock the head off a rattler one day with his Colt. Harman was also restless, and when Slocum told him about the job, he jumped at it. Then Slocum and Harman scoured the countryside for some more men. They wound up with five men. Bucky Bradley was an explosives man, and Slocum armed him with a case of dynamite. Then there was Tommy Holt, Esteban Morales, and Charlie Case, all good hands with their six-guns and rifles. Finally, there was Davey Pool, whose favorite weapon was his Bowie knife. They were a bunch of tough customers, all of them ready for a fight at the drop of a hat and all hungry for money. With expense money provided by Hodges, Slocum bought them all a good supply of ammunition. That was in addition to the dynamite he had purchased for Bradley. Food, water, a few bottles of good whiskey, bedding, tents and an extra saddle horse for the woman finished off the supplies.

After a few days on the trail, they had found themselves on top of a grassy and tree-covered hill overlooking the Big O Ranch. Slocum and Harman were bellied down on top of the hill. The others was back down on the other side with the horses. The road below them ran through an arched gateway with Big O in large carved letters on the arch. It roamed on a quarter of a mile to the front of the main ranch house, a two-storied monster with a covered porch running around the whole building. The cover of the porch was another, upstairs porch. Not far to Slocum's left from the ranch house, but back behind it, was a good sized bunkhouse. Nearby was a huge barn and a corral. To Slocum's right from the bunk-house, almost hidden from his sight by the main house, was a cook shack with a long extension that Slocum figured was the cowhands' dining room. Various other outbuildings dotted the area around and beyond the main house.

It was the middle of a workday, roundup time, yet there were plenty of horses in the corral. With all the hands out riding, that meant that O'Neill had horses a-plenty. The whole place had the look of money and power. Slocum wondered for a moment if he had done a smart thing by taking on this job, but then he thought about the ten thousand dollars he would pocket when it was over. He glanced over at Harman.

"What do you think, Gil?" he asked.

"I think we've took on a hell of a job," Harman said.

"You want to go through with it?"

"Hell yes. And I say there ain't no time like the present."

"How do you say we go about it?"

"We just ride down there, bust into the house, find the boss's lady and bring her out."

"Just like that?"

"Well, what's wrong with it?"

"Who do you reckon's in that house?"

"Hell, I don't know. Maybe O'Neill. But maybe he's out on the roundup with his boys. There might not be no one in there but women."

"Any hands in the bunkhouse?"

"I don't know what size his outfit is. There might be."

Just then a man with a rifle came walking around a corner of the house on the porch. He was looking around, vigilant.

"There's a guard," Slocum said. "Likely there's more. We got to plan this thing out."

Slocum decided they would spend a day or so just watching the house, sizing up the operation, and when they had the routine all figured out, they would make their plans. He left Harman and went back to join the others. He filled them in on what he had seen, and then sent a couple of them up to watch. For the rest of that day and night, he rotated the men, keeping watch. They gathered up the next morning to talk.

"There's four guards around that house all the time," said Charlie Case. "They's a mess of men in that bunkhouse, and they take turns."

"How many men, do you figure?" Slocum asked.

"I'd guess fifteen maybe," said Tommy Holt. "Maybe more."

Esteban Morales said, "I seen Julia, the boss's wife. She come out on the porch early this morning while I was watching."

"Are you sure it was her?" Slocum asked.

"It was her," said Holt. "I was watching with Esteban. I seen her too. I seen her plenty of times back before she was took off. It was her all right."

"How'd she look?" asked Slocum.

"What do you mean?" said Morales.

"Well, was she healthy? She look worried? Was anyone watching her to make sure she didn't try to run off?"

"She looked right at home to me," Morales said.

Slocum glanced at Holt, who just shrugged. Morales said, "I bet she don't look so smug when the boss gets her back home."

Slocum gave Morales a curious look. "Do you want to explain what you mean by that?" he asked.

"I don't mean nothing," said Morales. "Just the boss is gonna whip her good for running off again. That's all."

"He told me she was kidnapped," said Slocum.

Morales turned his head away, but Tommy Holt said, "Hell, Slocum, he ain't going to tell you that she run off with another man. She's his wife, and he wants her back. What do you expect him to say?"

Slocum leaned back against a tree and heaved a big sigh. He'd been had. He didn't really want to steal a woman away from where she wanted to be, not even for her husband. He must not have been much of a husband in the first place, or she would have stayed home with him. He was likely a brutal bastard anyway. This job suddenly took on a whole new character. He didn't like it. He thought about pulling out, but then he figured if he did, the others would go on without him. All of these men had worked for Hodges at one time or another. They had all been around these parts for a long time. Slocum was a newcomer. He was the only one who did not know the score, yet they had all readily agreed to ride with him. They didn't give a damn what happened to Mrs. Hodges when she got back home.

"Hell, Slocum," Morales said, "it ain't none of our business. She's the boss's woman."

"All right," said Slocum. "We'll sneak down there after dark. Take out those four guards without killing anybody. Knock them on the head and tie them up. That's all. Four of us will go to the house and take out the guards and get the woman. Two of you will watch the bunkhouse to make sure those guys don't come out, and one will stay with the horses."

For the rest of that day, Slocum worried about what he would do if they pulled the job off. If they got away safely with the woman, would he calmly deliver her back into the hands of the man she had escaped from? He couldn't stomach that. Something would have to be done. Yet he knew that he had to collect the money. These six toughs would have to be paid. There was no way around that. What would he do? What in the hell would he do?

When night fell, they moved down to the big gate. They rode a little farther toward the house, then stopped and dismounted. Slocum was more worried about Davey Pool and his knife than any of the others, so he told Davey to stay with the horses, all but one. He told Bradley to bring his horse along. Then the six of them moved on toward the house. Near the house, Slocum assigned Morales to watch the bunkhouse. Bradley's job was to move quietly, with his horse, to the corral. He was to wait until Slocum and the rest had brought the woman out of the house. Then he was to open the corral gate and run all the horses out. Slocum and the remaining three headed toward the main house. They split up, each one moving quietly through the night toward a different side of the house. As Slocum's man rounded a corner of the house, Slocum dropped down to his knees. He slicked out his Colt, then shifted it so that he was holding it by the barrel. He moved slowly and cautiously toward the porch. The guard stopped every so often to look around. Slocum was glad that the moon was hidden by lowering clouds. He inched closer. The man disappeared around the next corner. He would reappear soon. Slocum straightened up and ran for the porch. At the steps, he crouched down and waited.

Slocum took off his hat and placed it on the ground. He heard footsteps on the porch, and right away, the guard came back around the corner. He walked a few steps and stopped to look around. He moved on. He walked past the steps where Slocum was crouching on the ground. He stopped just at the top of the steps and looked around some more. Slocum held his breath. The man walked on, and Slocum moved quickly. He jumped up onto the porch and reached around the man with his left hand, clamping it over the man's mouth. With his right, he raised the Colt and brought it down hard on the man's head. The man collapsed, and

Slocum let him down easy onto the porch. He straightened up and looked around, and just then the other three men came around to the front.

"All took care of," whispered Gil Harman.

"Then let's go in," said Slocum.

He tried the door and found it locked. "Damn," he said. Without waiting for orders, Harman kicked in a front window and crawled through. In a minute he had the door opened, and Slocum and the other two hurried inside. It was dark in the house. Even so, Slocum saw the old man step out of a bedroom with a gun in his hand.

"Don't try it," Slocum said. "There's four of us." The old man hesitated. He lowered the gun. "Drop it on the floor," Slocum said. The old man let the gun fall. "Move over here."

Slocum gestured toward a large overstuffed chair, and the old man moved to it and sat down. "What do you want?" he said.

"Just keep quiet," said Slocum. "Gil, come over here and tie this old man up."

Harman went to work with his rope, and Slocum turned to the other two. "Find the woman," he said. They went running into various rooms. Soon Slocum heard a scream. Bucky Bradley came back into the main room with a kicking and screaming woman.

"That's my wife," said the old man. "Don't hurt her."

"Put her in that chair," said Slocum, indicating a straight chair standing against the wall, "and tie her up. And you keep quiet, ma'am. We don't mean to hurt anyone."

Charlie Case came out dragging another woman. She did not scream like the old man's wife, but she was fighting. She clawed Case's face, and the blood ran down his cheek and neck, staining his shirt collar. "I got her," he said. "I got the bitch."

Slocum moved quickly to grab the woman's arms. When he did, Case slapped her hard across the face.

"Do that again, Charlie," said Slocum, "and I'll kill you. Now tie her hands." He turned to the old man. "Are you Mr. O'Neill?"

"I am."

"Well, I'm sorry about this, but Mr. Hodges wants his wife back. We ain't hurt anyone. Not seriously." He turned back to Charlie Case and Mrs. Hodges and moved to help Case get her out the door. He was pleased to see that she had not yet undressed for bed. She was wearing jeans and shirt and boots. She was still struggling and kicking.

"Let me go," she said, "god damn you."

They got back outside none too soon, for the screams of Mrs. O'Neill had obviously awakened at least one of the cowboys sleeping in the bunkhouse. He had alerted the rest, and they were piling out the door, stumbling over one another, some with guns in their hands, all barefoot and in long johns, and all talking at the same time. Bradley had dropped the gate and was spooking the horses. The cowboys couldn't see anything but the horses running wild. Some of them ran after horses; others were looking around. Bradley mounted up and rode hard toward where Pool held the other mounts. Slocum and the men from the house hurried toward their horses. About the time they reached their horses and were struggling to get Mrs. Hodges mounted, one of the Big O hands realized what was happening.

"Hey," he yelled. "Over there."

Another cowboy, a gun in his hand, looked and fired a shot which went wild above the heads of the kidnappers.

"Hurry up," Slocum shouted, swinging up into the saddle of his big Appaloosa. Charlie Case was holding the reins of Mrs. Hodges's horse, and they took off as fast as the horses could run. Shots rang out behind them, but none hit their mark. It was dark, and the Big O cowboys were still confused, some still trying to catch horses, some hopping around one-footed, having stepped on sharp rocks, all of them talking and yelling at one another. Slocum moved out ahead of his crowd and rode under the arch in the gateway first. He turned toward the Hodges ranch. Looking over his shoulder now and then to make sure he was not leaving the rest behind, he moved fast.

When he had ridden about as far as he dared to ride a

horse hard, he slowed them to a walk. He spotted a hill not far ahead, and he led them up on top. Then he dismounted.

"What are we stopping for, Slocum?" Case asked. "They'll be coming after us."

"They'll be chasing horses for a spell," Slocum said. "We can see our backtrail for a ways from here. We'll rest up awhile. Unsaddle your horses and give them a drink. Let them graze. Esteban, you keep an eye on the trail. Someone'll spell you in a while." He walked over to the horse on which the woman was sitting and reached up to pull her off. She shrugged loose of his grip. He took her by the shoulders and turned her around. "Be still," he said, "and I'll untie you."

"Your kindness overwhelms me," she said, with an icy edge to her voice.

"We'll treat you the best we can, ma'am," he said, "but we got some hard riding to do."

He pulled the saddle off her horse and walked over to sit beneath a tree, leaning back against the trunk. He pulled a cigar out of his pocket and struck a match to light it. He watched as the cloud of smoke hovered for a moment, then dissipated in the slight evening breeze. He looked at Julia Hodges. She might have been thirty years old, certainly no older than that. And she was a good looker. He hated to think of Asa Hodges mistreating her. He tried to drive those thoughts out of his mind. "They're none of my business," he said to himself.

2

They rested up for a few hours and then saddled their horses and started riding again. They did not ride hard, for Slocum meant to save the horses. He had sent Tommy Holt back behind a ways to watch their backtrail. If Holt saw anyone coming, he was to ride hard, catch up and warn them. They had ridden about half the morning away before Slocum stopped them for a rest. He found a hilltop for them to stop beside. Down below the hill ran a little stream. It was enough for the horses to drink from. He had Esteban Morales build a small fire and cook them some food. It was a late breakfast. Holt caught up with them, and Slocum told him to get something to eat. Then he sent Charlie Case up on top of the hill to watch. Slocum filled a plate and carried it over to the woman, who was sitting slightly away from the men and pouting.

"Have some food, Mrs. Hodges," he said, holding the plate toward her.

She turned up her nose and looked away from him.

"Look," he said, "I'm sorry about this mess. I didn't know the whole story till I was way too far into it. The boss, your husband, told me you'd been kidnapped. That was all I knew, and I had no reason to doubt his word."

"And you do now?" she asked.

"Well, the men started talking. I got a different story."

"And what did they say?"

"Won't you take this?" he said, shoving the plate toward her again.

She took the plate and tried a bite.

"It sure won't poison you," Slocum said, "and you do need to keep your strength up."

"What did the men tell you about me?" she asked again.

"They said you hadn't been kidnapped at all. Said that the boss, Mr. Hodges, was, well, not the best husband. You'd most likely run off. That's what they said. Were they right?"

"Asa Hodges is an abusive son of a bitch," she said.

"And you did run off on your own?"

"I ran away in the middle of the night. I ran to Daryl O'Neill's ranch because of his son, Loren. Loren said that he wanted me. Even if I couldn't get a divorce."

"I see."

"Well, now that you know the truth, you'll take me back, won't you?"

"I'm afraid I can't hardly do that, Mrs. Hodges."

"I wish you wouldn't call me that."

"I'm sorry, uh, ma'am."

"You can call me Julia. That's my name. Why can't you let me go? If you don't want to take me back, just let me ride off. I'll make it back all right."

"Hodges promised a lot of money," Slocum said. "I'm afraid these boys wouldn't stand for it. And there'd be six to one. Like I said, I'm in this too deep to turn back."

"What's your name?" she said.

"Slocum, Mrs., uh, Julia. It's Slocum."

"Just Slocum?"

"My first name's John, but I usually just get called Slocum."

"Well, Slocum, how much money is Asa Hodges paying to get me back?"

"Ten thousand for me and another ten thousand for these boys."

"I suppose I should feel flattered," Julia said. "But the truth is he thinks he owns me, and he can't stand to be humiliated. So, are you sure the ten thousand dollars isn't what's making up your mind for you?"

"It's a lot of money for an old trail bum like me," Slocum said. "I'll admit that, and when he offered it to me to bring back his wife, who had been kidnapped, I went for it. But if I had known the truth, I wouldn't have."

"I don't know if I believe you or not," she said.

Slocum stood up with a sigh. "I guess it don't matter none," he said. "There's nothing I can do about it now anyhow except finish the job."

"You're a coward," he heard her say as he walked back toward the men. He tried to ignore it, but it cut deep. He was feeling like a coward, and he did not like the feeling. He walked into the circle of men and sat down. Some of them were still eating. Some had finished and were drinking coffee. Slocum had not told them yet about the whiskey he had stashed. He pulled a sprig of prairie grass and sucked on it till their was a lull in the small talk.

"Boys," he said, "when I took on this job, I thought the boss's wife had been kidnapped. That's what he told me. I didn't know the truth till you all spilled it the other night. What do you say we let her go back to the Big O and forget the whole thing?"

"You promised us sixteen hundred dollars each," said Davey Pool. "You gonna pay us that money if we let her go?"

"I ain't got it," Slocum said. "Hodges said he'd pay me when we got her back."

"Sixteen hundred dollars is a lot of money," said Morales.

Slocum glanced at Gil Harman. He knew Harman better than the others. They had been working together for some time now, and they had gotten along well. If anyone would go along with him, it would be Gil.

"She's going back to ole Hodges," Harman said. "One way or another."

"Over my dead body?" said Slocum.

"Slocum," said Harman, "I ain't never seen sixteen hundred dollars all at once in my whole life. I reckon if it came to a showdown, it'd be six against one. I hope it don't come to that. I kind of like you."

"Well, let's get riding," said Slocum. "Like you said, I promised you the money."

Just then Charlie Case came running down the hill and yelling as he ran. "Riders coming," he called out. "Riders coming."

"How many?" Slocum asked.

"I'd say about twenty."

"Get mounted," said Slocum.

"We can hold them off from this hill," said Morales.

"I don't want to kill anyone if we don't have to," Slocum said. "Let's get going."

They mounted up and started riding hard. Slocum held the reins to the horse Julia was on. He didn't want to give her a chance to ride away from them. They moved into a deep valley sheltered by high rocky bluffs on both sides. Slocum rode up beside Case and handed him the extra reins. "Take these," he yelled, "and keep going. Gil, let's you and me slow them down." He slowed his big Appaloosa, and Harman slowed his horse as well. The others continued riding hard ahead.

"What you got in mind?" Harman said.

Slocum looked around. "Let's get our horses hid in behind them rocks," he said. "Then we'll climb up yonder with our rifles."

"Two against twenty?" Harman said.

"We'll be hid and we'll catch them by surprise," said Slocum. "Come on."

"Well, shit, why not?" said Harman, and they rode their horses behind the big rocks and tied them there. Then, taking out his Winchester, Slocum started climbing. Harman followed him. About halfway up the rise he indicated a spot behind a boulder.

"Right there," he told Harman, and Harman snugged down. Slocum kept climbing. He found himself a spot above Harman and to his right. Then he settled down to wait and watch. "Gil," he called out. "Can you hear me?"

"I hear you," Harman answered.

"Try not to kill anyone."

"Shit. We're outnumbered ten to one. How the hell are we going to stop them without killing anyone?"

"I don't know," Slocum said. "Just do your damndest."

It wasn't long before the riders appeared in the distance. Slocum cranked a shell into the chamber of his Winchester and called out again to Harman. "Gil."

"Yeah."

"Wait for my first shot."

As the riders drew closer, Slocum took careful aim. He waited. Then he took a deep breath and squeezed the trigger. The blast echoed through the valley, and the bullet kicked up dust just in front of the riders. The horses neighed and reared as their riders hauled back on the reins. Some of the men pulled guns and looked for a target. A man in the lead called out, "Take cover." Slocum fired a second round into the dirt as the riders below dismounted and scampered for places in the rocks to one side of the valley or the other. Harman fired a couple of shots into the ground. Soon all of the riders were hidden. Their horses milled around loose in the valley.

"You down there," Slocum yelled.

"Who are you?" came a response.

"Never mind that," called Slocum. "We don't want to kill anyone. Just move out and catch your horses. Turn around and ride back where you came from. No one will get hurt."

"Fat chance" was the answer, and it was followed by a gunshot. Then it seemed that all twenty of the Big O cowhands started shooting. Bullets ricocheted around the rocks near where Slocum and Harman were secreted. Each man hunkered down low behind his sheltering boulder. In a couple of minutes, the shooting slowed, then stopped. The valley seemed deathly quiet.

"Slocum," came the voice of Harman in a harsh whisper.

"What?"

"What do you say now?"

"Let's spook their horses."

The two men began firing shots, kicking up dirt near the feet of the milling horses. The Big O men fired back.

Slocum and Harman had to duck down for safety now and then. Slocum looked around for another spot to run to. He found one and ran crouching for it. Then he fired some more shots. Harman was firing again. The cowboys below were still firing back. Soon, however, all twenty horses had turned and run back in the direction they had come from. Slocum started down the hill. "Let's go, Gil," he said, as he approached Harman's hiding place. "It'll take them a while to round up their critters."

They hurried back down to where they had tied their own horses, mounted up and rode hard into the valley and after the rest of their bunch. A few shots were fired after them, but they went wild and wide. Glancing over his shoulder, Slocum could see the cowboys running after their horses. Slocum and Harman rode hard till they could no longer see the cowboys behind them. Then they slowed their pace.

"Well, you pulled that off, ole buddy," said Harman.

"Yeah. We did all right that round," said Slocum.

They rode for a while before they picked up the pace again. The valley narrowed just ahead of them, and soon they spotted Julia and the other five dismounted and resting on the valley floor. Once again, Julia was seated away from the men. Slocum and Harman rode in and dismounted.

"We heard shots," said Morales.

"What happened?" asked Case.

"We just slowed them down a bit," said Slocum. "We'll get started again soon as we rest our horses."

He sat on the ground, leaned back against a boulder, took out a cigar and lit it. He exhaled in a loud sigh.

"What happened back there?" asked Case again.

"Oh, hell," said Harman, "we just scared them into dismounting, and then we scared their horses off."

"That's all?" said Morales. "You didn't kill no one?"

"Slocum told me not to hurt them none," said Harman. "We just had us a little Sunday school is all."

"Well, I'll be shit," said Morales.

"Then we've still got twenty men on our ass," said Tommy Holt.

"We're well ahead of them," Slocum said. "Relax."

"Relax, shit," said Holt. "You should've knocked off at least a few of them. Cut down the odds some."

"We'll be back at Hodges's place long before they catch up with us," Slocum said.

"You just god damn better be right about that," Holt said, pacing angrily away.

When Slocum had finished his cigar, he figured his and Harman's horses had rested long enough. He called out for everyone to mount up once again, and they started riding. They rode at an easy pace. There was no sense in wearing out the horses. He was pretty sure that they were well ahead of their pursuers. They rode to the end of the valley, and Slocum called a halt. He rode up beside Bucky Bradley and turned to look at the valley walls.

"Bucky," he said, "do you think that you could block that valley with some dynamite?"

Bradley looked up at the rocky walls and grinned. "Yeah," he said, "I could do that easy."

"Get after it then," Slocum said. "We'll wait for you up ahead."

Bradley dismounted and started digging into his saddlebags while Slocum led the rest on ahead. Bradley worked fast. Soon he was climbing the wall to his left. He went up close to the top, to a carefully selected spot, and he placed his charge underneath the edge of a large, precariously perched boulder. He trailed fuse all the way back down as he descended to the valley floor again. Then he studied the other side. He looked back to where he had placed the first charge. Then he looked again to the other side. He pointed one way and then the other, and then he made his decision. Taking another load of material with him, he started to climb again, this time just opposite where he had gone before. The climb this time was a little more difficult than the first. He slipped a time or two, but at last he made it to his chosen spot. He planted the explosives and started back down, once again, trailing fuse. Finally he was back down. He stood for a moment studying the walls. He was satisfied. Taking out a match, he knelt down beside the end of the fuse on the north side of the valley. He struck the match. It went out.

"Damn," he said, tossing it aside. He took out another match and struck it. It flared up, and he lit the fuse. He waited to watch it begin to fizz. Then he quickly mounted his horse and raced to the other side. Dismounting, he found the other fuse and dropped down near it. He took out another match, scratched it against a rock and touched the flame to the end of the fuse. It caught. It fizzed. Bucky ran to his horse and swung into the saddle. Turning it out of the valley, he whipped it into a run. He looked over his shoulder. He looked back ahead. He could see Slocum and the others waiting for him on the prairie beside the little stream near a clump of trees.

Just then a loud blast shook the ground. Bucky's horse reared and jumped sideways. He fought to control it and make it move forward, and then a second blast roared. When Bucky managed to get some control of his mount back, he looked over his shoulder again to see great clouds of dust and debris flying through the air. Even through the dust, he could see great boulders tumbling down the sides of the walls toward the valley floor below. He grinned and urged his horse forward. In another couple of minutes, he dismounted and ran toward Slocum, a wide smile across his face.

"How was that?" he said.

Slocum grinned and slapped him on the shoulder. "Just fine, Bucky," he said. "You did just fine. I don't think anyone will be riding through there for some time now."

The others ran to Bucky, closing close around him, pounding his back, shaking him by the shoulders. "God damn, Bucky," said Case, "that was like a damned earthquake."

"I blew the son of a bitch all to hell, didn't I?" Bucky said.

"You damn sure did," said Morales. "I never seen nothing like that."

Slocum glanced over at Julia. She was sitting alone in silence, the only one not elated by the blasts. He walked over to sit beside her.

"You think you've stopped them," she said, "but you haven't."

"I hope you're wrong," he said.

"I'm not," she said.

Slocum hesitated a moment, and then he asked, "You love him that much? That O'Neill kid?"

"He loves me that much," Julia said. "He was my way out. My escape from Asa. Me? I hate Asa that much."

3

There was no way through the valley after the job Bucky had done on it, no way any time soon. Even so, Slocum wanted to get some distance between them and the Big O hands. He had them all mount up and ride, and they rode away the rest of the daylight hours, stopping again beside the ambling stream for the night. Slocum allowed a fire to be built and had Morales fix some coffee and prepare a hot meal. He smoked and had a cup of coffee while he waited for the food. The men were loud and boisterous, but he figured there was nothing he could do about that. Julia was seated off some distance from the men again. Slocum was alert enough to make sure that she was on the opposite side of the men from where the horses were picketed. If he wasn't going to keep her close, he at least wanted to make sure that she couldn't get to a horse without being seen. He posted a guard just to make sure. Then he dropped off to sleep.

It was not a restful sleep. It was filled with images of a battered Julia, her eyes blackened, blood running down from her lips, her clothes ripped to shreds. He saw Asa Hodges punching her. He tossed and moaned out loud. No one heard him though. The rest of the men were sleeping some distance away, and several of them were loud snorers.

While Slocum slept thus fitfully, Julia sat up and watched. Charlie Case, standing guard, was down by the stream. When

Julia was fairly certain that the rest of the men were sleeping, she stood up. She waited for a moment to see if anyone noticed her. Then she started to walk, slowly and carefully. She managed to creep past Slocum. He groaned and rolled over, and she stopped, startled, but he did not wake up. She moved on. It seemed to Julia that it took forever, but she got past the sleeping men, her eyes flicking from their prone forms to the erect form of Case by the stream.

She made it to the horses, and there she wasted no time. Quietly she tossed a blanket over the horse she had been riding. He nickered and stamped, and she whispered to him to calm him. She adjusted the blanket. Then she heaved the saddle up on his back. She bent over to reach under his belly for the cinch strap, and suddenly she felt hands grab her by the waist and pull her back. A man's crotch was pressing against her rump and grinding. She straightened up and tried to turn, but the hands held her hard.

"Let me go," she said.

One hand came up and clasped itself over her mouth. The voice came in a harsh whisper. "You ain't going no place, lady."

She struggled as the other hand slid from her waist around to her belly and then up to her heaving breasts.

"Calm down, lady. No one has to know."

She tried to stomp on his feet.

"Be nice, lady. I won't hurt you."

She opened her mouth and bit down hard on his hand. "Ahhh," he cried, jerking his hand loose. She turned to face him, and he grabbed her shoulders, pushing her back against the horse. The horse fidgeted, but he managed to hold her against it. Suddenly she felt the sharp tip of a knife blade against her throat.

"I told you to be still," said Davey Pool. "Now if you don't mind me, I'll just cut your throat."

Esteban Morales sat up from his sleep. "What's going on over there?" he said.

"Mind your own business," Pool snarled over his shoulder. That was enough to wake Slocum. He stood up and looked around. Taking in the situation in a hurry, he ran over to where Pool was holding Julia. Taking Pool by a shoulder, Slocum spun him around and smacked him on the side of the head. Pool fell back against the already fidgeting horse. With his left hand he wiped at the place where Slocum had hit him. His right brought up the knife, ready to fight.

"Keep out of this, Slocum," he said.

"Davey," said Slocum, "get out there and relieve Charlie."

"I ain't taking no more orders from you, Slocum."

"All right," Slocum said. "Have it your way." He turned as if to walk away, then spun back around quickly, grabbing Pool's right wrist and holding it tight, while driving his own right deep into Pool's gut. Pool lost all of his wind and dropped the knife. Slocum brought up a knee, smashing Pool's face. Then he grabbed Pool's shirt and slung him to the ground. Julia quickly bent down to pick up the knife. She held it behind her back. Pool groaned and got to his knees. He wiped at the blood on his face with a sleeve.

"You broke my nose, you son of a bitch," he said. "You broke my fucking nose."

"Saddle up your horse and get out of here," Slocum said.

"You owe me money."

"Not anymore I don't. Saddle it up."

Pool already knew that he couldn't whip Slocum, and neither man had his gunbelt strapped on. He got to his feet groaning and managed to get his horse saddled. He turned to walk back toward where he had been sleeping, but Slocum stopped him.

"Get on and ride away from here," Slocum said.

"I got to get my gun and my bedroll," Pool protested.

"You don't have to get anything," said Slocum. "Just mount up and get out."

"You can't turn me loose out here with no gun. I could die out here like that."

"If you don't get going, I'll turn you loose naked."

Pool hesitated.

"I mean it," Slocum said. "Or I could just kill you right here."

Pool looked in desperation toward the other men. All of them were up and watching.

"You best move on out," said Gil Harman.

"Ain't nobody here going to do nothing to help you," said Morales. "We got no quarrels."

Pool felt the empty scabbard where he kept his knife and realized that he did not have it, but he thought better of saying anything about it. Grudgingly, he mounted up, turned the horse and started riding. Everyone watched as he disappeared from sight.

"Slocum," said Morales. Slocum turned to look at him. "He'll be seeing you again. You might not see him though. He'll be coming up behind you."

"He can try it," Slocum said. He turned toward Julia. "And you can get back over there where you belong."

"I suppose you think I owe you some thanks," she said.

She tossed her head and started to walk past him, but as she did, he grabbed her by the arm, forcing her to turn. She gave him a hard look. Slocum held out his hand.

"You can give me that pig sticker," he said.

She slapped the handle of the knife in the palm of his hand and stalked away. Slocum walked to a nearby tree. With all his might, he stabbed the knife deep into the trunk of the tree. Then he pushed the handle sideways until the blade snapped. Leaving half the blade in the tree, he tossed the rest away. Walking back to his bedroll, he took a cigar out of his pocket. As he went past the men, Morales said, "He'll just get another one."

"Fuck Davey Pool," Slocum said. He sat down and dug out a match. He wasn't sleepy anymore. "Morales," he said, "since you're so damned alert, go relieve Charlie."

Morales stood up with a grin. Taking his rifle, he said, "Okay," and headed toward the stream. Slocum lit his stogie. He could feel Julia's eyes burning into the side of his head. He tried to recall if he had ever felt so hated, and he could not. He didn't blame her either. She had every right to hate him. He just about hated himself. No, he told himself, she sure didn't owe him any thanks. It was his business to control these worthless bastards he had gathered up to do this dirty job.

Julia got up and moved over to sit beside Slocum. He braced himself for a tongue lashing, but she just sat silent for a long moment. Then, "Slocum," she said, "I really should thank you for what you did. I'd have been raped if you hadn't stepped in."

"I wish I had never taken this job," he said. "If I had known the whole truth, I wouldn't have."

"Asa would just have found someone else to do it," she said. "It's not your fault. Not really. And you did it without killing anyone. Another man might not have been so careful about that."

"Well, it's only five against one now," he said. "Maybe I can figure a way out for you. Get you back to the Big O where you want to be."

"I don't want to be at the Big O," she said.

Slocum gave her a surprised look.

"I don't love Loren O'Neill. He's better than Asa. That's for sure. But I don't love him."

"Well, what do you want to do?"

"I want to go back to Pennsylvania. That's where I come from. I have family back there. Asa came out there on a trip to buy some horses from my daddy. That's where we met. He was nice there. He pretended to be. When he got me away from home, though, it didn't take long for him to show his true colors. I don't like the West, Slocum. I want to go home."

"It sounds like we're caught between a rock and a hard place," Slocum said. He had been thinking that one way to solve the problem would be to somehow allow the Big O boys to catch up with them. Then he could just say that they were too badly outnumbered, and they would have to let Julia go back to Loren O'Neill. "Won't O'Neill let you go home?" he asked her.

"No," she said. "He won't. I said he's better than Asa, and he is, but he won't let me go."

Slocum couldn't think what to do. Now he really had a problem. On one side was Asa Hodges. On the other

O'Neill's men. Both wanted Julia, and Julia didn't want either one. How in the hell, he asked himself, did he get himself into these messes? It was greed. That's all it was. He'd been thinking that with that ten thousand dollars, he could lay around and play around for a good long spell. That's what caused it. But then he decided that he was glad to be in this position. Here was a woman trapped. She wanted out, and until he'd stumbled into the picture, she was all alone. Okay. Maybe it was a tough position to be in, but at least she wasn't in it all alone. Not anymore. Slocum stood up suddenly.

"Get ready to ride, boys," he called out.

"It's awful early, Slocum," said Gil Harman. "Can't we at least get some coffee?"

"Go ahead and make it," Slocum said. "But be packing and getting saddled up."

Pretty soon the horses were all saddled and packed and the coffee was made. They drank some, and Morales stuffed the pot and cups into his pack. Slocum kicked out the fire.

"Mount up," he said.

They rode slow and easy in the early morning darkness. A whippoorwill sang its mournful song off in the distance. Soon the sun peeked up over the edge of the horizon, and Slocum picked up the pace a little.

"We keep riding like this," said Harman, "we'll be back at the ranch by tomorrow evening."

"Yeah," Slocum said, and he glanced at Julia. Her face was long.

"And then we'll get all that *dinero*," said Morales.

"I'm going to get drunk for a week," said Bucky Bradley.

"I'm sure as hell going to quit my job," Harman said.

Tommy Holt said, "I'm going to get me two whores at the same time, and—"

"Shut up," Slocum said. "There's a lady with us."

"Oh," said Holt. "I'm sorry as hell. I didn't realize she was a lady. All I knowed was that she's married to one man and run off to live with another one. I'm sure sorry I didn't know she was a lady."

"Tommy," said Slocum, "you've got more money coming

to you than you've ever seen before. You don't want to spoil it now by getting yourself killed, do you?" He moved his Appaloosa to one side and turned to face them. They all halted their mounts. Then the rest moved aside, away from Holt. Holt sat alone, nervously facing Slocum.

"I just don't think that you oughta be telling us what to say and what not to say," he stammered.

"I don't want you to say anything for the rest of the ride," Slocum told him. "Not one word."

Holt cocked his head, looking sideways at Slocum. Slocum saw his hand move slightly toward his six-gun.

"Go for it," Slocum said. "I'd like nothing better."

"You're a bastard, Slocum."

"I told you not to talk."

Holt reached for his shooter, but Slocum got his out first, and he fired just as Holt was raising his gun. The shot tore into Holt's chest and ripped out his back. Holt jerked. His face took on a surprised, stunned look. His hand relaxed and dropped the gun. He leaned back a little and then fell forward onto his horse's neck. The horse stamped around nervously, and the dead body slid off to one side, landing hard in the dirt. Slocum glanced at the other four riders. They just sat still in their saddles. Gil Harman shrugged.

"You want us to bury him, Boss?" asked Case.

"You can if you want to," Slocum said. "I'm riding on."

Case looked down at the lump that had been Tommy Holt. He tipped his hat and rode past it. Slocum was already riding ahead, Julia riding beside him. Slocum called out over his shoulder, "One of you catch up that horse." They were well out ahead of the others, and Slocum spoke out of the side of his mouth to Julia in a harsh whisper. "It's four to one now."

Julia had been startled by the killing, and she was more than a little shaken up, but she managed a little smile in spite of everything. She knew by this time that Slocum really was on her side. She wondered if he would kill the other four men and take her away. She wondered if he would give up ten thousand dollars for her. That was a lot of money. The other four men had caught up with them. Esteban Morales was saying,

"You know, now there are but four of us to split the ten thousand. That's more better. What does that make for each of us?"

"That's twenty-five hundred dollars each," said Gil Harman.

"Twenty-five—You mean two thousand and five hundred?"

"That's right."

"Two thousand and five hundred dollars," Morales said. "I don't know what I'll do with that much money."

"If it's worrying you, you could give me your share," said Charlie Case.

"I think I'll keep my worries," Morales said, "and my money."

Harman urged his horse up beside Slocum. "Say," he said, "you don't mind if we talk, do you?"

"Not at all," said Slocum. "Just remember the lady."

"None of us ever forgot," Harman said. "Just Tommy. He won't forget again."

"Two thousand five hundred dollars," Morales said. "How much is that in pesos? Do you know?"

"I ain't worrying about the pesos," said Gil Harman. "I'm watching that god damned cloud up ahead."

Slocum had been watching too. It was one big white puffy cloud that appeared to be sitting on the ground up ahead. It was huge on the bottom and tapered off at the top. Right through the middle, another cloud, this one a long strip horizontal to the ground, sliced its way through the monstrous one. It meant there was a hell of a storm brewing.

Just then they rounded a bend, and Slocum drew back on the reins, halting the Appaloosa. Everyone else stopped with him. Up ahead, blocking their way, were fifteen riders lined up side by side. Each one held a rifle across his saddle.

"I thought they were trapped in the valley," said Bradley. "They couldn't have got through there."

"It ain't the same ones," Harman said.

"What?"

"O'Neill split his men into two teams. Somehow this bunch swung around wide and got ahead of us while the other bunch followed us."

"That's Loren in the middle," Julia said. "With the big white hat."

Slocum heaved a big sigh. "Well," he said, "now it's fifteen to five. The odds keep shifting."

Esteban Morales said, "Uh oh."

4

"What do we do, Slocum?" Harman said. "There's too damn many of them for us to fight."

Just then Loren O'Neill hollered from the other side. "Hey, whoever you are. Let the woman go, and you can ride out of here with your lives."

"I see my fortune blowing away in the wind," said Esteban Morales.

Heavy drops of rain splattered on the ground and on the hats and shoulders and backs of the men. The raindrops were few and far between, but they were signs of more to come. The puffy white cloud suddenly changed color. It had turned a dark gray and was spreading out. Soon the sky would be dark. A long streak of lightning slashed through it in the east. Slocum thought fast. There was nothing ahead but fifteen hostile riders and a hell of a storm. They were headed due east. Behind them was the closed-up valley with another fifteen or so men on the other side of the pile of rocks Bucky Bradley had created with his blasting. There was no road going north and south. To the north was prairie, which, if they were to turn northwest, would lead them into the high hills. To the south was more prairie and more high hills. The chances of escaping the storm looked better to the north. Slocum did not want to totally escape it. It might just be their savior.

"When I say go," Slocum said, "turn north and ride like hell."

"Well," O'Neill yelled again, "what do you say? You don't have a chance. Might as well give it up and save yourselves."

The sky opened up all at once and torrents of rain began to slash down. The wind blew it sideways. "Go," Slocum called out, and they all turned and headed north, Slocum holding the reins to Julia's horse. Glancing over his shoulder, he could barely see the others. It was certain that O'Neill and his riders would not be able to see them. Lightning crashed all around them. It was dark as night. Slocum's hope was that they would lose their pursuers in the storm and then ride it out. In the flash of a bolt of lightning, he saw a grove of trees ahead to his left, the west.

"Head for those trees," he called out, just as the first hailstones started to fall. One hit him in the back. He thought of Julia. Her head was unprotected. He maneuvered her horse up beside his and handed her his hat. "Here," he said. "Put this on." They had almost made it to the trees when a large hailstone smacked him on top of the head. He felt the pain, and then he felt dizzy. He wobbled in the saddle. He fell, splashing in the water that was standing on the ground, and then he blacked out. The rest rode into the trees to wait out the storm.

If anyone noticed that Slocum was missing, he did not say anything. No one talked to anyone else. The storm was still raging, and even though the trees gave them some shelter and comfort, it was still too loud for conversation. Lightning flashed and thunder crashed nearby. Hailstones sometimes found their way through the branches of the trees overhead. Only Julia knew that she was no longer being led. She thought that perhaps Slocum had turned loose of her reins when they headed into the trees. She had not actually seen him fall. She looked around a bit to see if she could spot him, but the driving rain and the hail made her, like the others, mostly hunker down and look at the saddle horn.

She swung down out of the saddle and found the trailing reins, which she lapped around a low branch. Then she took the blanket roll off the horse's back and untied it. She unrolled the blanket with no regard for what was inside, and then sat down beneath a tree and pulled the blanket over her head. She would worry about escape when the storm was past. Not far away, each of the men had done the same thing.

Gil Harman sat beneath a tree with his blanket over his head, but he was holding it up with his arms in front of his face and squinting out into the rain, trying to see someone else. He saw a horse not far away, but he could not tell whose it was. "Can anyone hear me out there?" he yelled. "Hey. Anyone." There was no answer. The raging storm was just too loud. Finally, he gave it up and relaxed his arms, allowing the blanket to fall over his face. He had made it to the trees, and at least one other had. He saw the horse. Likely they were all in there.

The hail stopped, and so did the lightning, but the rain kept falling sideways due to high wind. It kept up the rest of the day and throughout the night. The sun rose the next morning in a bright blue cloudless sky. The only evidence of the savage storm the night before was the soaking ground, fallen branches and the soppy clothes of the riders. Esteban Morales was the first one up and looking around.

"Hey, where is everybody?" he cried. "Slocum? Gil?"

"I'm here," said Bucky Bradley. He came walking between the trees, leading his horse.

Gil Harman appeared then. "I wouldn't go yelling around too much," he said. "That Big O bunch might be somewhere around."

Charlie Case showed up with two horses and Julia. "I found her," he said, "but I didn't see Slocum."

"He's around somewhere," said Harman.

"But he had the woman," said Morales.

Harman looked accusingly at Julia. "Where'd he go?"

"I don't know," she said. "When I rode into the trees, I was alone."

The men looked at one another, uncertain what to do. "Oh, hell," said Bradley, "he'll show up pretty soon."

"What if he don't?" Morales said.

Harman shrugged. "We'll just have to go on without him," he said.

Julia was hoping he'd show up, and real soon. He was the only one of the bunch who had any real sympathy for her situation. She had no idea what he might do about it, if he did show up. Still, he was her only hope. She did not really want to return to the Big O, and she damn sure did not want to go back to Asa Hodges.

"Esteban," said Bradley, "can we have some coffee?"

"We'd better not build a fire till we have a look around," said Harman. "No telling where those Big O boys are at."

Case walked to the edge of the woods and looked out. Everything was quiet. The sky was clear. "I see a hill out there," he said. "Maybe someone could ride up there and have a look around."

"Go ahead," said Harman. "Have at it."

Case looked for a moment as if he wished he had kept his mouth shut. Then he shrugged and went for his horse. The poor beast had not been unsaddled all night, but Case swung into the saddle and kicked it in the sides. Cautiously, he rode out into the open. Looking around as he rode, he made his way slowly toward the hill.

"Do you think they're still out there?" Julia asked.

"There ain't no telling," said Harman. "If they are, ole Charlie's good as dead."

"Yeah?" said Morales. "What about the rest of us?"

Case made the top of the hill and spent some moments looking all around. At last he headed back to the others in the trees. Dismounting, he said, "I didn't see nobody. I could see a long ways in every direction, but I never seen no sign of them."

"Of course," said Morales, "you couldn't see on the other side of these trees, could you?"

"Well, no. Not really."

"Hell," said Harman. "Go ahead and see if you can find any dry wood. These horses need to be unsaddled for a spell anyhow. They need a good rest."

It took a while, but Morales at last got a small fire going,

and then he soon had coffee boiling. The horses were grazing on the lush, wet grass. Everyone got a cup of coffee.
Morales squatted by the fire. Julia leaned back against a tree.
Bradley and Case sat on the wet ground, and Harman walked
around, looking out over the plains. He finished a cup of
coffee and then went digging into his saddle bags for some
dry clothing. He walked behind a large tree to change. The
rest followed his lead. Then Bucky Bradley, the smallest of
the bunch, looked at Julia.

"My clothes might come close to fitting you, ma'am," he
said. "I got another set of clean ones if you want to try."

"Yes," she said. "Thank you."

In dry clothes, they all had another cup of coffee. "So,"
said Julia, "what are you planning to do with me?"

"Just what we started out to do," said Harman.

"What if you run into Loren and his boys?"

"We'll just have to do our best to avoid running into
them," Harman said.

"Like the plague," Morales added. "Like the black
plague."

"Or the boobonic," said Charlie Case.

"If you head straight back to the ranch," Julia said,
"you'll run into them for sure."

"There's a little town called Bentley about a day's ride
north of here," Harman said. "We'll head up that way. We
can get rested up, get some new supplies and then head east.
We'll sweep a big circle around and go back down to the
ranch from east of it. O'Neill won't hardly figure us for
that."

"That'll take more time," said Case. "Won't it?"

"About three more days, I figure," said Harman.

"Three extra days of riding," said Bradley. "I don't like it."

"You want to run into those fifteen cowboys?" said Case.
"I damn sure don't."

"You could just turn me loose," Julia said. "That would
solve all of your problems."

"But then, señora," said Morales, "we would also be turning loose of all that money."

"Say," said Case, "if Slocum ain't with us, you reckon we'll get his share too? How much do you reckon he was going to get paid?"

"I don't know," Harman said. "When we get her home, we'll just have to deal with Hodges. That's all."

"He'll pay you as little as possible," Julia said. "He's a real tightwad."

"Gil?" said Morales.

Harman stroked his chin and paced about. He turned to face the others, a wide grin on his face. "What if we don't take her back?" he said.

"What do you mean?" asked Case.

"What if we get back close to the ranch and find us a good place to hole up? Then one of us goes to the ranch. He tells Hodges that we got his wife, and if he pays us enough money, we'll get her back to him. How's that sound?"

"Well," said Morales, "he did tell Slocum that she had been kidnapped."

"Hell yes," said Bradley.

"How much do you think we should ask him for?" said Case.

Harman turned toward Julia. "How much?" he asked.

"Oh," she said, "I'd say at least a hundred thousand."

"Dollars?" said Morales.

"Not pesos," said Julia.

"A hundred thousand?" Harman said. "Does he have that much?"

"Of course, he does," Julia said. "Why do you think I married the son of a bitch? He's got it all right. Make him pay through the nose."

"All right," Harman said. "Let's get these horses saddled and get on the way."

"We heading for Bentley?" said Case.

"That's right," said Harman. "That'll be our first stop."

As Julia watched her horse being saddled, she thought about her predicament. She knew that Asa did not have a hundred thousand dollars. But he would have a hell of a time convincing these men of that. They would insist. He would offer less. They would argue. It would delay things for a while at least, and she would have more time to try to figure a way out. She damn sure did not want to be returned to Asa Hodges. In just a few more minutes, they were saddled up, packed and headed north.

Slocum's horse was wandering. The big Appaloosa was disoriented after his night in the frightening storm. Saddled and with his reins trailing, he moved slowly. He was confused. The man should be on his back, or else he should have taken care of him, putting him up in some warm place for the night. Instead the horse had been turned loose to roam alone in the dreadful fury of the raging wind and rain. Now it was over, but he did not know where he should be. He grazed some, but mostly he wandered. He sniffed the ground. He lifted his head and sniffed the air, looking around.

Half-conscious, Slocum rolled over. His face rolled into a puddle of water, and when he tried to suck in a breath of air, he instead gargled water. He coughed and lifted his head. Slowly, the events of the day before came back to him. He remembered the Big O riders and the big storm. There had been hail. He had been racing for the shelter of a grove of trees, and he must have been hit by a large hailstone. He rolled over on his back again and looked up at the clear sky. He wondered how long he had been unconscious. He located the sun in the sky and knew that it was still fairly early in the morning. He was soaking wet, and he felt as if he had been beaten all over with big sticks.

He tried to sit up, and he fell back moaning. He managed to roll over onto his side, and then get himself to his hands and knees. With much effort, he at last got to his feet. Pain shot through his body. He realized that if he had indeed been knocked silly by a hailstone and then lay there all night, he had been pummeled all over by hundreds of the damn things. He looked around and saw nothing of any note other than the grove of trees ahead. He started walking. Each step was a misery. A time or two he almost fell, but he managed to keep going. At last he reached the grove. He felt like sitting down, but he was afraid to. He thought that he might not be able to get up again.

He looked around and saw nothing. He decided to wander more through the grove and see if there was anything to see there. He found some horse shit that was fairly fresh. They must have spent the night in here for shelter from the storm. He continued searching. He found another place where a horse had been. Then he came across the spot where Morales had managed to start a fire. Of course it could have been someone else, but he was almost certain that it had been Julia and his companions. There was not enough sign for it to have been the fifteen Big O cowhands, and it was highly unlikely that anyone else had been riding out this way when the storm hit.

They had lost him in the storm, and then sometime in the morning, they had decided to just ride on ahead. He tried to decide whether or not they had abandoned him. They certainly had not looked hard for him, if at all. Well, he would deal with that issue when he found them. They couldn't be too far ahead, but then, they were riding, and he was on foot. He did not know this country well, but he believed that there was a small town somewhere to the north. They might be headed there. He studied the wet ground until he was fairly sure they had indeed ridden north. There was nothing for it but to follow them, so he started walking. It would take him a hell of a long time to get anywhere. He did not know how far it was to the town, and it would be an easy thing to miss it, to bypass the town altogether never knowing, and to wander in these empty plains until he just dropped dead. He had nothing except his Colt, and he was walking slow.

He figured that he had walked about a mile to the north of the grove of trees. The cool morning aftermath of the storm had vanished, and the hot sun was warming the day quickly. Slocum's wet clothes were beginning to dry. Up ahead, he saw a line of scattered and scrubby trees, and he knew that there must be a stream there. He walked toward it. He could use a drink of water and a brief rest in some shade. He was beginning to wonder just how long he would be able to keep this up. His hat was gone, and the sun was beating on his head unmercifully. He remembered that he had given the hat to Julia to protect her from the hailstones. He at last made it to the tree line. He could hear the gurgling water just ahead. Then he heard another sound. It was the nicker of a horse. He could scarcely believe it. He wondered if he would be able to catch up a loose horse, and he wondered if it might be a horse with a rider. It could even be his lost companions. He hurried ahead. The ground dropped off to the water, and as he was about to start going down the slope, he saw the horse at the water's edge. It had been drinking. It raised its head high and whinnied in recognition. It was his Appaloosa.

5

Slocum could scarcely believe his good fortune. He made over the horse for a few minutes before unsaddling it. Then he checked his saddlebags and found clean clothes. He changed. He found a dry rag and wiped his Colt down. Then he took the Winchester out of the saddle boot and gave it a good going over. He even found some coffee and a pot. He found dry cigars and matches, and he fired one up. Then he built a small fire and made some coffee. He washed his face as best he could in the stream, and then he just sat and smoked and drank coffee, relaxing, trying to get some strength back after his long ordeal. His body still ached from the long pummeling it had taken and from the long morning walk, but he was beginning to feel somewhat better. At last he put out the fire, saddled the Appaloosa and mounted up. He still had a long ride ahead of him, and he didn't even really know where he was going.

There was still some trail sign, and Harman and the boys still seemed to be headed north, perhaps to the small town up that way. Slocum could not recall its name. He had never been there, only heard of it. It was supposed to be a very small place with no law other than the nearest county sheriff, who was several miles away. There was no sign of the fifteen riders from the Big O. They were probably somewhere along the road to Hodges's ranch waiting in ambush.

Of Slocum's own gang, or what was left of it, Harman had the most sense. He likely figured the fifteen would be waiting along the road and had decided to swing north and then east. Slocum would have done the same thing. It was a way of getting around the ambushers and back to Hodges's place safely. At least it was possible that it could work that way.

He rode easy. He didn't figure himself to be too far behind the others, and there was no need to wear out his big stallion. Harman would be taking it easy as well, he figured. As he rode, he thought about Harman, Bradley, Case and Morales. He wondered it they had taken any time at all to look for him, or if they were deliberately trying to cut him out of this deal. It would be interesting to find out when he caught up with them. He could have a fight on his hands. It was also still quite possible that he would run across the Big O boys again. That could be a hell of a fight. Finally, he wondered what he would do if he managed to get Julia back to Hodges. He didn't really want to turn her over to the son of a bitch. He might have yet another fight on his hands there. Well, he told himself, he would just deal with each situation as it came up. He rode on.

As Harman and the others approached the tiny town of Bentley, they came across an abandoned house. They decided to check it out. It was a two-room house, one room being a bedroom and the other serving for everything else—living room, kitchen and dining room. It was dusty and filled with cobwebs, but other than that, it was serviceable. A table and four chairs sat in the middle of the main room. There was a woodstove in the kitchen. There was no other furniture. Harman suggested that they stop there and rest for a night, maybe longer. They took their bedrolls inside. Harman said that Julia could stay in the bedroom. The rest of them would sleep in the main room.

Morales gathered some wood and built a fire in the stove. He put on some coffee right away and then went about scaring up some food for them. Outside, the others unsaddled all the horses. Harman said that they could go into town, one or two of them at a time. They would have to keep Julia out of town though, so at least two of them would stay out at the house with her at all times. If they took her into town, she might say something and get some help. They couldn't take that chance. They finished the meal that Morales had prepared, and Harman announced his intention to ride into Bentley and check things out. Case said he wanted to go in with him. That left Morales and Bradley to stay at the house and watch Julia. Harman thought that was good. Morales and Bradley could keep each other from getting any wild ideas about the woman. They saddled two horses and headed into Bentley.

"Well," said Morales, "we might just as well settle in for a spell. Anyone want some more coffee?"

"I'll take some," Julia said.

"I'd sure like a drink of whiskey," said Bucky Bradley.

"Hey," said Morales, "we got some whiskey. Slocum packed some in before we left, but we never got a chance to drink any of it."

"Well, by God," said Bradley, "we got a chance now, ain't we?"

"I'd say so."

In no time at all, Morales had dug out a bottle of the good bourbon whiskey. He wiped out a couple of tin coffee cups and poured them full. Then he glanced over at Julia. "You want some?" he asked her.

She pushed her coffee cup across the table toward him. It was still half full of coffee. "I'll take some in here," she said. Morales filled the cup the rest of the way with whiskey. Bradley took his first drink.

"God damn," he said. "That's good stuff."

Morales sat down and took a drink. "It's wonderful stuff," he said.

Julia sipped at her mixture and said nothing, but it did feel good after the ordeal she had been through. Well, she hadn't just been through it. She was right in the big middle of it. Still, the whiskey was good. It would help for a little while, but she had to be careful. She did not want to get drunk. If she could encourage these two to keep on drinking, maybe they would get drunk. Maybe they would get so drunk, they would pass out. The other two had gone to town. She could saddle a horse. She could get away from them. But if she did manage to do that, where would she go? She would have to keep heading north, away from Asa Hodges and away from the Big O boys, away from these four, maybe five. She wondered how Slocum was doing, if he was dead or alive. She had no idea how far away the next town to the north was, but she decided that it would be worth the try. If only these two would drink themselves into oblivion, she would do it.

Harman and Case rode into Bentley. There was not much to it. The main building in the town was a huge combination saloon and general store. There were a few other buildings, but it was hard to tell what they were used for or if they were even in use anymore. There were a few horses in front of the saloon. They tied up there and went inside. They found themselves in a well-stocked general store. No one was in there. They had gone through the wrong front door. There was a connecting door in the wall though, so they walked through there. There were about six men in the room besides the barkeep, and most of them had the look of cowhands. Two of them though, old men who looked more like hide hunters, sat at one table by themselves. Although there were plenty of tables available, the other four all stood at the bar drinking. They all looked in the direction of the newcomers, strangers in town. Harman looked the room over and nodded at the two old men.

"Howdy, strangers," one of the old men said.

"Howdy," Harman answered. Then he glanced toward those at the bar and nodded to them. They returned the nods, and a couple of them said out-loud howdies. The barkeep looked at Harman and Case. "What can I do for you boys?" he said.

"Can we get a bottle and couple of glasses over here at

this table?" Harman said, jerking a thumb at a table close to the far end of the bar.

"Sure thing," said the barkeep.

Harman and Case took seats where they could watch the room. Harman was wondering if any or all of these men could be Big O riders. He did not really think so. If they had been, chances were there would have been fifteen of them and not just six. The whole country was cow country, so it was not unusual for a saloon to have cowhand customers. The barkeep brought the bottle and glasses, and Harman paid for it. He poured the two glasses full and shoved one toward Case. He had just taken his first sip when he heard the sound of a door shutting. He glanced toward the top of a stairway at the far end of the room and saw a woman coming down. She was dressed in the gaudy clothes of a saloon gal, and Harman felt something stir inside of him. He had been riding the range now for several days with a good-looking woman he could not touch. He kept staring at the woman on the stairs.

She walked slowly down, studying the small crowd of men below. When she reached the bottom, she walked over to the bar, where she was met by the barkeep. "I see we got some new blood in here, Mac," she said.

"Yeah," Mac said. He nodded toward Harman and Case.

"You know them?"

"Never saw them before, but that one in the white hat bought a whole bottle."

"Give me a glass," she said, and Mac shoved a glass toward her on the bar. She took it and turned to stare at the two strangers for a moment before walking to their table. "Buy a girl a drink, cowboy?" she said.

Harman stood up quickly, removing his hat. "Sure," he said. He reached over to pull out a chair, the one right next to his. "Sit down," he said. The girl sat, placing her empty glass on the table. Harman sat down again and poured her glass full.

"Thanks," she said, and she took a healthy gulp. Harman

scooted his chair closer and reached an arm around her shoulders. She looked at him and smiled.

Back at the house, Bucky Bradley was swaying in his chair in a drunken stupor. Morales was singing a Mexican song and waltzing alone around the floor. Julia still sipped her first drink and watched carefully. Morales seemed as if he might go on and on like this. Bradley had just about had it. He would pass out real soon. She reached for the bottle and made out like she was pouring herself another drink. Then she held up the bottle and looked at Morales.

"You ready for another one?" she asked.

He waltzed to the table and held his glass down. She poured it full. He took a long drink. "Hey," he said, "what about my ole pardner here? Bucky, you need more drink?"

Bucky muttered something unintelligible.

"He needs some more," Morales said, and he dragged Bradley's glass across the table. Julia poured it full, and Morales shoved it back to Bradley, who picked it up, wavering about and in danger of spilling it, but he managed to get it up to his lips for another drink. He put the glass down and lurched to his feet. "Got to go outside," he muttered, and he weaved his way to the door, barely staying on his feet. He hit the door with both hands, and it swung wide open. He fell out on the porch, and the door banged closed again. Morales was waltzing and drinking. Julia wondered how much longer he could last.

In the saloon in Bentley, Gil Harman still sat with his arm around the girl. She sipped her drink and looked up at him admiringly. Case was watching them and feeling left out. "What's your name, cowboy?" she asked. "Gil," he said. "What's yours?" She snuggled against him and said, "Sugar Tits will do just fine. That's what they mostly call me around here." Gil pulled her closer. "Well, Sugar Tits," he said, "that's a pretty good name. Now give me a little kiss." She tilted her head back, and he leaned down toward her. Their lips met and lingered for a moment. "I've got a nice room upstairs," she said. "You want to go up there with me?"

Gil stood up and pulled her chair back. He helped her to her feet, and as she was turning to lead the way, Gil looked down at Charlie Case. "Guard that bottle," he said. "And don't look so glum. You'll get your turn."

Sugar Tits took Gil by the arm and led him to the stairs. They climbed slowly to the top, the girl cuddling against him all the way. Case watched them go, and when they disappeared down the hallway upstairs, he drained his glass and poured another drink. Sugar Tits took Gil to a room down the hall and opened the door. A lamp was burning on a table, its flame turned down low. She let go of Gil's arm and walked across the room to the bed. Turning to face him, she smiled, and she reached behind her with both hands to unlace her bodice. Gil took off his hat and stuck it on a peg on the wall. Then he unbuckled his gunbelt and draped it over another hook there. He walked over to a chair and sat down to pull off his boots.

Sugar Tits was slipping out of her flimsy dress. Gil watched her as he stood up to pull off his shirt. Her hair was blond with a tinge of red, and it hung down to her shoulders in wavy locks. She had a pretty face, which he thought couldn't have been thirty years old, even though it did show some wear. But she had a nice inviting smile, and as she dropped her dress to the floor and then stepped out of it, he could see that her skin was smooth all over. He stripped out of his jeans and walked over to her in his long underwear. He was unbuttoning his long johns, and she reached out to help him. She was beautiful, he thought, standing there watching her, naked and helping him to get that way. In another minute, he stepped out of his long drawers, and his rod was already standing up and throbbing. Sugar Tits looked down at it.

"Ooooh," she said, and she reached for it and took hold of it in her right hand. "It's bucking like a bronc."

"It's raring to go," he said.

Sugar Tits walked toward the bed, pulling Gil along by his convenient handle. At the bed, she still held on. She crawled in and dragged him in after her. She was on her back, her legs spread wide. Gil took a good look at the amber bush that grew just above her crotch and noticed that the curly hairs seemed to be damp. She pulled him between her legs and guided his tool into her waiting slot, and he drove it in deep.

"Oh, yes, Gil," she said. "Fuck me. Fuck me hard."

He pounded away for all he was worth.

"I will," he said. "I am. Oh, God, that's good."

Morales almost ran into a wall with his waltzing, and to avoid smashing into it, he did a twirl, but as he spun, he lost his balance and fell over backward. He landed hard on the floor, dropping his glass of whiskey. He raised his head and looked at the poured-out stuff on the floor. "Oh, hell," he said. "What a waste." He started to get up but fell back again, and then he decided that it was just too much trouble. He relaxed and closed his eyes, and he was out in a minute. Julia sat still a bit longer watching him. When she was sure he was gone, she stood up and walked over to him. Carefully, she reached down and withdrew the six-gun from his holster. She got Slocum's hat and stuck it on her head, and then she opened the door slowly. Just outside the door, Bucky Bradley was laid out on his face. She took his gun as well and hurried on out to the horses. As quickly as she could, she saddled the horse she had been riding. A Henry rifle was in the saddle boot. That was good. She started to mount up, but she had a second thought. She went back into the house quietly and found the food Morales had brought in. She rolled most of it into a blanket and went back out. Tying the blanket roll on securely, she mounted up and turned the horse north, riding away from her latest captors.

Slocum was tired and hungry and very sore. He had been on the trail now for several days. He had pulled off the rescue of the woman, although it was now doubtful if it had indeed been a rescue; he had outrun one gang of pursuers only to run smack into another bunch; he had been running from them when the hailstorm struck; he had been knocked out and pummeled by hailstones for hours, only to wake up alone in a puddle of water on the prairie and then have to walk for several miles before finding his horse again. After all that, he had been in the saddle for several more hours. He did not want to think how long it had been since he had eaten. His stomach knew though, and it was trying its damndest to tell him.

Some miles back he had lost any more sign of a trail, but he continued north. He was pretty sure that he was headed for that town. He couldn't think of its name. As far north as they had gone, that was about the only place they could be headed. They could have turned east already and headed back for Hodges's ranch, but he didn't think so. As he rode along, he kept watching in all directions for any sign of either his own party or of pursuit by any of the Big O bunch. He saw no one though. It was as if he was the only man on the face of the earth. And then he came to a road.

It wasn't much of a road, but it was a road, and all roads lead somewhere. He figured this one would lead him to Bentley. Ah, yes, Bentley. That was the name of the little town. It had just popped back into his mind. Bentley. But which direction was Bentley? The road ran more or less east and west. He sat still in middle of the road thinking. He looked at the tracks in the dirt, and he saw what appeared to be the tracks of five horses moving east. That could be his bunch. They seemed to be the freshest tracks on the road. They had been put there after the rain. Of course, they could be tracks of four cowhands from someplace or other headed into town to get drunk, but he was following four horses, and there were no other tracks, none that had been made since the rain. It was a good chance, and he decided to take it. He turned east on the road.

It was getting to be late in the day. Soon it would be dark. He hoped that he would come across his gang or come to Bentley before it was too late to keep traveling. He was ready for a stop, for some food and for a good rest. There was still a lot of riding ahead for him and perhaps a fight or two along the way. He was about to stop and make camp for the night when he saw the little house beside the road. It was dark, but he could see a wisp of smoke trailing out of the chimney. Either someone was there, or someone had been there recently. When he reached the house, he saw two horses standing there that seemed familiar. He stopped in front of the porch and was trying to decide whether to yell out or to go up and knock on the front door. He thought that he would take a closer look at the horses, but just then he noticed the body lying on the porch.

6

Slocum slipped out his Colt as he backed his Appaloosa away from the house, back into heavier darkness. When he reached a distance far enough away from the house to feel somewhat secure, he dismounted and started moving slowly toward the house. There was a body on the porch. No telling what had happened in there. He had to be careful. He reached the porch, hearing no sign of life other than the relaxed blowing of one of the horses. He looked at the body on the porch, then at the front door and finally over at the two horses. He moved closer to the horses. He was certain that they belonged to his bunch. He moved on back to the porch and stepped up beside the body there. Rolling it over, he saw that it was Bucky Bradley. Then the reek of whiskey reached his nostrils, and Bucky groaned. He was not dead, he was dead drunk. Slocum stood up and stepped over the body of the drunken Bradley and up to the door.

Still holding his Colt ready, he reached for the handle. He found the door just barely shut, not latched, and he gave it a shove. It opened easily. Slocum stepped inside. He saw Morales lying on the floor, and he saw the cup beside him. The smell of whiskey was strong. Slocum looked around. He saw the bottle on the table. There were two more cups on the table as well. He walked over there to check them. One still had some whiskey in it. The other was over half-full of coffee and whiskey. He checked the other room and found it empty. "Damn," he said, shoving his Colt back into the holster.

He walked over to Morales and nudged him with the toe of his boot. "Morales," he said. "Morales." Morales groaned and stirred, but he was too far gone to respond. Slocum stepped back out onto the porch and squatted down to shake Bradley, but the results were no better with Bradley than they had been with Morales. He stood up and tried to think. What could have happened? They had all been separated by the storm the night before. Perhaps these two had somehow found each other and not the rest. But there were three cups. Who had used the third one? There were three cups, but only two horses and two riders. Where were Harman and Case and Julia, and who had been the third drinker? Had it been one of the missing three? He tried Morales and Bradley again, again with no results. He would just have to let them sleep it off.

He went back outside and walked out to his horse. Leading the big stallion to the house, he unsaddled it and left it with the other two horses. Then he took the saddle and bedroll into the house and went into the bedroom. He fixed himself a place on the floor. Walking back into the other room, he found a little food, and he found some coffee in a pot. There was still some fire in the stove, and the coffee was still hot. He found a cup and poured himself some. Then he sat down to drink it and gnaw at the food. When his stomach at last felt better, he went into the bedroom to get some sleep. There was nothing else he could do anyway until morning.

In Bentley, Harman woke up to discover that he and Case were both in bed with Sugar Tits. Sugar Tits and Case were still asleep. All three of them were naked as jaybirds. Harman rubbed his eyes and realized that it was morning. He sat up slowly on the edge of the bed and looked for his clothes. He pulled on his jeans and then reached over Sugar Tits's sleeping form to nudge Case.

"Charlie," he said. "Wake up."

Case moaned and tried to roll over, but there wasn't room. He rolled the other way and rolled right out of bed, falling hard on the wooden floor. "Damn," he said. He sat up on the floor, looking around to get his bearings. The noise woke up Sugar Tits, and she sat up rubbing her eyes. Her makeup was smeared and her hair was frazzled. Harman thought that she had looked much better the night before. She saw Case getting up off the floor.

"What happened, cowboy?" she said. "You fall off the bed or get bucked off?"

Harman was pulling on his shirt. "Come on, Charlie," he said. "We got to get back."

"What's the hurry?"

"They'll be wondering what come of us," Harman said.

Case found his clothes and started to get dressed. Harman was ready to go. Sugar Tits looked at him. "Don't forget my money," she said.

"Oh, yeah," Harman said. "Hurry up, Charlie."

Case was sitting on a chair pulling on his boots. He glanced over at Sugar Tits. "I sure did have me a whopping good time last night," he said. "I ain't never had a better."

"Come on."

"Okay. Okay." Case headed for the door, which Harman already had open.

"Leave my money," said Sugar Tits.

Harman dragged Case out the door. "Let's get out of here," he said. They hurried to the landing and started down the stairs. The saloon was practically empty. One drunk was sitting at a table, his head down. There was no one else in sight. Harman and Case hit the floor and headed for the front door. Sugar Tits appeared at the top of the stairs with a sheet over her shoulders.

"Hey, you cheap bastards," she screamed. "What the hell are you trying to do? Pay me, god damn it."

Harman hit the front door, but it opened in instead of out, and he bounced back and fell on the floor. Case gave him a hand and helped him to his feet. They looked up at the landing. Sugar Tits had disappeared. The two cowboys managed to get outside and run for their horses just as she appeared in an open window upstairs. The sheet had fallen away. She was still naked, but she was holding a six-gun and aiming for them. Case saw her and screamed, "Look out, Gil."

Harman looked up just as Sugar Tits fired. "Yow," he said, as the bullet whizzed over his head. "Let's go." Quickly, they mounted their horses, which had been waiting patiently at the hitchrail all night long, and turned them to race out of town with bullets flying all around.

Slocum woke up early and rolled up his blankets. Then he went back to the other room and fixed some more coffee. There was still a little food left, and he ate enough to hold off hunger. Morales and Bradley were still out. He checked the amount of whiskey left in the bottle and figured they'd had enough to keep them out for at least half of the day. He tried to wake them up anyway, and he did come a little closer to it than he had the night before. Bradley raised his head but let it drop again. Morales moaned and rolled over. Slocum decided that they wouldn't either one of them be worth a shit to him anyway. He walked over to where the horses stood grazing and he checked over the ground.

There had been five horses there. All of them had been together. All five of them. And now there were but two. What had happened? If Morales and Bradley got drunk, and the others did not, perhaps Harman and Case had just decided to abandon them there. It could have happened that way. He studied the ground some more. Two horses, it seemed, had ridden back out to the road, but the third horse had headed north across the plains. He followed the horses that had gone to the road and discovered that they had turned east. He had already figured that to be the way into Bentley. But why had the third horse gone north? He tried to think it all through and consider the various possibilities. The five of them had gotten together after the storm, and they had come across the house and decided to stop there for a spell. Then Morales and Bradley had gotten drunk, and the other three had left them there, two heading into Bentley and the third riding north.

It didn't make sense. Had one of the men taken Julia to town? Why? And why would the other one ride north? Maybe he was scouting for Big O riders. The other possibility was that two of the men had gone to Bentley, and Julia had ridden north. They wouldn't have let her go—unless, Harman and Case had gone to town, leaving Morales and Bradley to watch Julia, and Julia had escaped after those two passed out. He decided to leave the two drunken wretches where they lay and follow the trail north. It was the only thing that made any sense.

It took only a few minutes for the town of Bentley to come awake following the gunshots. And it took a few more minutes for Sugar Tits to tell the men what had happened. Soon six men from the saloon were dressed, armed and mounted. They took off following the trail of the two deadbeat trail bums.

Morales finally woke up. He sat up on the floor and rubbed his eyes, moaned and held his head. At last, he stood up on uneasy legs and went to find the coffeepot. The stove was cold, so he got some sticks out of the wood box and built up the fire. He still had a canteen full of water, and he put on a pot of coffee to boil. Then he started looking for food to prepare for breakfast. He scratched his head in puzzlement. He knew there had been more food. What could have happened to it? He shrugged and went ahead with what he had.

Out on the road from Bentley, Harman and Case were riding hard. Case came up beside Harman and yelled loud as they rode. "How come you didn't pay that gal?"

"I didn't have no more money," Harman answered.

"Oh, shit," said Case. "They're going to hang us for sure."

"They got to catch us first."

•   •   •

Morales poured himself a cup of coffee in the same cup he had used for whiskey the night before. He sat down at the table and took a first sip. He moaned with pleasure and relief. He looked around and realized that he was alone. He guessed that the woman was still sleeping in the other room. But where were his partners? Slowly he remembered that Case and Harman had gone into town, but he thought they should have been back long ago. He and Bradley had stayed behind with the woman. So where was Bradley? He took another sip of hot coffee, put the cup down on the table and stood up with a groan. He walked to the door and opened it, and saw Bradley stretched out on the porch. He glanced to the side and saw the two horses there. Two? There should have been three. He kicked Bradley, who woke up with a snort and sat up quickly, pulling his gun and looked around for a fight.

"Hey, Bucky," Morales said. "Wake up. There's only two horses."

"Huh?" Bradley uttered.

"Look over there. Two horses. There should be three."

"Three?"

"Yeah. You, me, and the woman. Three horses. Gil and Charlie ain't come back from town. Still, there should be three."

Bradley struggled to his feet and looked at the two horses as if they could tell him something. "Well, where's the woman?" he said.

"Asleep in the other room," said Morales. "I didn't want to bother her so early yet."

"Come on," said Bradley, pushing himself past Morales to go through the door. Morales followed him into the house and across the room, where Bradley shoved the other door open and stepped into the room. It was empty. No woman. No bedroll. Nothing. "She ain't here," he said. Morales stepped in to look for himself.

"She's gone."

"That's where her horse is at," said Bradley. "She took off on it. Whyn't you watch her?"

"Well, why din't you?"

"We better get after her. Gil and Charlie will kill us."

"We can't go yet," said Morales. "I just got coffee made and breakfast started."

Bradley looked around, confused. "Well," he said, "give me a cup of that coffee."

Harman and Case were riding hard, too hard. Their mounts were getting winded, and Case's horse stumbled. Case tumbled. Looking over his shoulder, Harman saw what had happened. "Damn," he said. He slowed his horse and turned, riding back for Case. Case was on his feet as Harman rode up beside him reaching out a hand.

"Catch my horse," Case said.

"We ain't got time for that. Get on."

"That thing can't carry both of us, not riding hard like we was."

The six Bentleyites came barreling at them. Harman drew his revolver, and Case pulled out his own. The Bentleyites started firing. Bullets kicked up dust nearby and whizzed by the heads of the two fugitives. Harman quickly raised his hands, dropping his gun. "Don't shoot," he screamed. Case dropped his gun and raised his hands high. The six riders stopped shooting and rode up, each of the men holding a gun on their two captives. Two of the six were the two old men Harman had noticed in the saloon the night before. One of the old men looked down at them. "I'm Olaf Johnson," he said. "What are your names?"

"Gil Harman," said Gil.

"Charlie Case."

"Well, Gil and Charlie," said Johnson, "these here are my brother Sven, Maxie, Slick, Jugs and Callaway."

"Pleased to meet you fellows," said Case, forcing a grin.

Harman nodded.

"I just thought we had all ought to know each other before we go and hang you boys," Johnson said.

"Hang us?" said Case. "What for?"

"What for?" said Johnson. "You just spent the entire

night with Sugar Tits, the both of you, and then you went and run out on her without paying. That's a dastardly deed, and it calls for harsh measures."

"Well, maybe it's pretty bad," said Harman, "but it sure ain't no hanging offense."

"It is in Bentley," said Sven.

"But, uh, we, we ain't in Bentley no more," said Harman. "Can't we talk this over?"

"Maxie," said Johnson, "catch up Charlie's horse for him. He'll need him to set on when he gets strung up."

Maxie rode off after Case's horse.

"Now, just a minute there, Olaf," said Harman. "You don't want to hang us. Why, hell, all we done was to just screw a whore."

"All night long," said Callaway.

"You robbed the lady," said Johnson. "And raped her."

"Raped?" said Case.

"She was expecting to be paid for her services," Johnson said. "You made use of her services and never paid. That's the same as rape, and that's a hanging offense."

Maxie came riding back with Case's horse, and Johnson ordered Case to mount up. Case did, but with some difficulty, as his legs were growing weak and rubbery. Johnson was looking around. He spotted a suitable tree not too far off.

"Come on," he said. He led the way, and Jugs and Callaway took the reins of Harman's and Case's horses and brought them along. Soon the hands of the two hapless cowhands were tied behind their backs and two ropes, each with a hangman's noose tied to its end, were thrown up and over a long and sturdy branch.

"Hey," said Harman, "you're just teasing us, ain't you? You ain't really going to do this? Are you? Are you?"

"Are you?" said Case.

"Go ahead, boys," said Johnson.

Two of the men rode up beside the cowboys and slipped the nooses over their heads.

"You got any last words?" Johnson asked.

"We didn't really rob the gal," said Harman. "We was going to come back and pay her."

The four younger Bentleyites laughed. Sven Johnson snorted. "Why didn't you just pay her before you left then?" asked Johnson.

"Well, we ain't got no cash on us just now," said Harman.

"But you were going to get some and come back and pay," said Johnson. "Go on, boys. Slap their horses' asses."

"No. Wait," Harman shouted. "Listen. We're on a job. It's going to pay real well when we're done."

"How well?" Johnson asked.

"Ten thousand, maybe more," said Harman.

"Tell me about it, boys," said Johnson, his old, rheumy eyes starting to gleam.

7

Slocum did not ride hard. He figured that he was not too far behind Julia, and he figured further that Julia would not be able to ride very fast. He did not think that she really knew where she was going. In fact, Slocum did not know where she was going. She was headed more or less north, and that was likely all that she knew. Her trail was easy to follow, and he expected to catch up with her before the day was done. The only thing that was worrying him was what he would do when he caught up with her. He guessed that he would still have to take her back to Asa Hodges, even though he found the thought of that to be detestable.

Julia kept thinking that there had to be a town somewhere ahead. Or a road. If only she could come across a road. All roads lead somewhere. She did not think that Asa would have any men looking for her to the north, and surely Loren O'Neill would be concentrating on the trail between the two ranches. She ought to be able to get to a town with a stage line that would lead her to a railroad. She had no money, but she would worry about that later. She would find a way. She just had to get away from those two men, Asa Hodges and Loren O'Neill. Let them all kill each other fighting over her. She didn't give a damn. The only one of the whole bunch who was almost worth a damn was that Slocum, but he had made a bargain with Asa and with those other men, and she was pretty damn sure that he would keep his word, however reluctantly. She kept riding and kept hoping to see a town or a road.

Morales and Bradley were just finishing their morning coffee. "There's enough food here yet for us to have some breakfast," Morales said.

"I told you we ain't got time for that," said Bradley. "If Gil and Charlie get back from town and find out that we lost that woman, they'll have our hide. We got to get after her."

"Oh hell, all right," said Morales. He finished his coffee and tucked the cup into his saddlebag. Bradley finished his and handed the cup to Morales, who packed that one as well. He started gathering up the remaining food and utensils.

"Leave all that stuff," Bradley said. "We'll come back for it after we catch the gal."

They grabbed up their packs and went out to the horses. They were saddling up when Bradley noticed the tracks. "Hey," he said, "someone else has been here. Look. Whoever it was, he come in and then he followed Mrs. Hodges. See there?"

"You are right, compadre," said Morales. "We better catch him up and find out who it is."

"Right over there is the house," said Gil Harman. "That's where she is."

"Wait a minute," said Johnson. "Is them your two pals you said you left with her?"

"Yeah," said Harman.

"It's Bradley and Morales," said Case.

"They're mounting up to ride," said Johnson. "Looks like."

"There's just two horses, Olaf," said Sven.

"There ought to be three," said Harman.

"Come on," said Johnson. "Let's find out what's up."

"Hey, Bucky," said Morales. "Look what's coming."

Bradley and Morales saw the six riders from Bentley and

their two partners come riding hard at them. The six had out their shooters. "I told you they'd be pissed off," said Bradley. "Let's get the hell out of here." They mounted up fast and headed north. The riders from Bentley started shooting.

"Hold your fire," Johnson shouted. "Don't kill them. They know where the woman is at. Sven, keep after them. You and Maxie and Slick. The rest of us is going to stop and check out the house."

As the three rode hard after Bradley and Morales, Johnson stopped with the others, including Harman and Case, at the house. "Jugs," said Johnson, "go on and peek inside." Jugs dismounted and went cautiously to the door. He shoved it open and stepped inside. At the same time the others got off their horses, but Johnson walked over to where he had seen Morales and Bradley mounting up. He studied the ground for a while. "There's been at least six different horses here," he said, looking accusingly at Harman and Case.

"There was five of us rode in here," Harman said. "The four of us and the woman."

"So who was number six?" the old man asked.

Harman shrugged. "I don't know," he said. "There was another one with us, but we lost him the other night down south in the storm. Never seen him again. I don't think it could have been him. We was all together. He'd have stayed with Morales and Bradley if it'd been him."

Johnson stepped up onto the porch and walked to the door and inside. Jugs was standing in the middle of the room. Johnson nodded toward the door on the other side of the room. "Did you check in there?" he asked.

"No."

"Well, go check it, dummy."

Jugs walked on across the room and stepped through the door. He found an empty room. He turned around a couple of full circles, then walked back out. "Nothing in there," he said.

Callaway came into the house behind Harman and Case. Harman looked at the empty bottle on the floor. He stepped over to the table and found the cup of cold coffee with whiskey poured in it. He picked it up, sniffed it and put it back down. Case was looking at the leftover food and the utensils. "I'd say they took off in a hurry," he said. Harman bent to pick up the empty bottle. He held it out toward Johnson.

"What it looks like to me," he said, "is that Morales and Bradley went and got drunk. Whenever they passed out, the woman run off."

"Jugs," said Johnson, "grab up all that grub and bring it along."

Without another word, he led the way outside and back to their horses. They mounted up and followed the tracks north.

Bradley and Morales rode hard to the top of a hill. They stopped and turned to look back, and they saw the three men pursuing them. "They're getting closer," said Morales. "There's only three of them though. Let's lay an ambush right here and kill them dead."

"You sure?" said Bradley.

"You want them to catch us and kill us dead?"

"Hell no."

They dismounted and moved their horses back a ways, and Bradley reached into a pouch of his saddlebags and pulled out a stick of dynamite. He looked at Morales, and they both grinned. They ran back to the edge of the hill where they had first stopped and lay down on the ground. They could see the three riders coming. Bradley fixed a fuse and then cut it short with his penknife. "You got matches?" Morales said.

"I always got matches," Bradley said, and he pulled three out of his pocket.

"Light the son of a bitch," said Morales nervously. He looked from the stick of dynamite to the riders and back again.

"Ain't no hurry," Bradley said. "We got a short fuse here."

The riders came closer. Morales was sweating. "Now?" he said.

"Not just yet," Bradley said. "I'll just let them get to the bottom of the hill."

"Holy Jesus," Morales said, and he pulled out his six-shooter and cocked it, just in case. The riders were almost to the hill when Bradley at last struck a match. It flared up and went out. "Damn it," he said. "Oh shit," said Morales. Bradley struck his second match with the same results. He put the dynamite on the ground and took off his hat. He struck the third match under the cover of his hat and held it for a moment. It was burning nicely, and he touched it to the fuse, which caught and fizzed. "God damn it," said Morales. Bradley picked up the stick, held it for a moment, looked down at the riders about to start up the hill and finally tossed it. Morales put his face in the dirt and his hands over his head. Bradley watched the flight of the deadly stick as it arched up high.

Sven, in the lead, saw the dynamite. He saw the sparks on one end. "Oh hell," he said, trying desperately to turn his horse. He ran into Maxie's horse, knocking it down and sending Maxie tumbling. The dynamite hit the ground and bounced once before it blew. The explosion was deafening, and the air was filled with flying debris.

Back down the trail toward the abandoned house, Johnson and the others heard the blast. "What the hell was that?" said Jugs.

"It was dynamite, you fool," Johnson said. "What the hell else could it be?"

"It was Bucky," said Harman.

"What?"

"Bucky Bradley," Harman said. "He was our blasting man. He closed a valley back west and cut off fifteen men that was after us."

"Well then, he's likely just cut off three more," Johnson said. "Let's go."

The air cleared a little, and Bradley and Morales could see three horses down, two men on their backs and another standing, looking dazed. Bradley pulled out his six-gun and fired, dropping the man. "Now let's get out of here," he said.

Morales stood up and looked at the devastation down the hill. "Holy mother fucker," he said. "You sure did stop them all right."

"Come on," said Bradley. They ran back to where they had left their horses. They could only see one, and he was skittish. "God damn," Bradley said.

"We should have tied them better," said Morales. "The blast spooked them."

"Let's catch this one," said Bradley. He started to run toward the horse, but Morales stopped him.

"He's already spooked," he said. "Go easy."

"All right. All right. You go that way."

Morales moved to his left and Bradley to his right. They walked slowly around the nervous horse. At last, Bradley began moving toward it. It stamped its hoofs and snorted. Bradley stopped. The horse stood still. Morales moved in toward it. It turned and ran, moving north. "Damn it," snapped Bradley.

"Hey," said Morales. "Talk nice. He can hear you."

Julia came across a nice spot beside a clear running stream. The ground was grassy, and it was shaded by a small grove of trees. She was saddle weary, and she had not seen anyone coming up behind her on the trail. She figured the horse needed a rest too, so she stopped and let the horse drink and graze. She too drank deeply. Then she pulled off her boots and stuck her tired feet in the cool water. She lay back in the grass to relax.

In a few more minutes, she got up and walked over to the horse. She took off the blanket roll and moved back over to a smooth spot on the ground where she rolled it out and found the food she had stashed there. She got a piece of beef jerky and a chunk of bread and started to eat. It wasn't the best meal she had eaten, but she was hungry, and it was good. Then a voice startled her.

"I'm pretty damn hungry," it said. "I hope you got enough there for the both of us."

She turned quickly and saw Davey Pool standing there snarling down at her.

Pool ate his fill and washed it down with gulps of water. Then he reached for Julia. "We'll just finish up what we started the other day," he said. She struggled as he pulled her close to him, and as his lips sought hers, she turned her head from one side to the other. "Stop it," she said. "Stop it. You don't have time for this."

"I got all the time in the world, you bitch," he said.

"No, you don't. The others are after me."

He backed off and looked at her. "Who?" he said. "Who is it that's after you?"

"The Mexican," she said, "and the one you called Bucky. Charlie and Gil probably, and maybe even Slocum."

"How'd you get away from them?" he asked.

"During the storm," she said. "We all got separated. Then they found me again in the morning. All but Slocum. We didn't see him. The others took me with them, and we stopped at an abandoned house just outside of Bentley. Gil and Charlie went to town. They left the Mexican and Bucky to watch me. Then those two got silly drunk and passed out, and I ran away. You know they're after me. I'm worth too much money to them."

"Yeah," said Pool. "To me too. If I can get you back to old Hodges first, he'll pay me."

"That's right," she said, "and you won't have to split it with anyone."

Pool stood up. "Get this shit rolled back up and tied on your horse. We're riding out of here."

Julia breathed a sigh of relief and got herself busy with the blanket roll. Once more, she had been lucky. She wondered how much longer her luck would hold.

Morales at last got the horse by its neck. It bucked and stamped a little. He stroked it and talked softly to it to calm

it down. Finally, it stood still. Then he mounted and went after the other horse. In a short while, he and Bradley were
back on the trail.

Johnson found the carnage left by Bradley's blast. He found
Maxie with a broken leg and Slick just waking up from a
stupor. He also found the body of his brother, Sven, with a
bullet hole in its chest. One horse was dead, and the other
two were badly hurt. He told Jugs to finish them off. Standing over the body of his brother, he said, "You two, Harman
and Case, bury him."

They dug a shallow grave with knives, and when they had
buried the body, they piled stones over the grave. When they
had finished the job, they were exhausted. They sat down on
the ground and wiped their brows with their sleeves. "Can
we have a drink of water?" Harman asked. Johnson ignored
the question and turned to Callaway, who had been tying up
Maxie's broken leg. "Them two ain't going to be worth
nothing to us for a spell," he said. "Put them on these two
horses and head them on home."

"Hey," said Harman, "those are our horses. What—"

"You won't be needing them no more," Johnson said. He
pulled out his old Remington revolver and fired two shots,
one into the chest of Harman, and one into the chest of Case.
Both men fell over dead.

"You want we should bury them, Mr. Johnson?" Jugs
asked.

"Hell no," said Johnson. "Buzzards needs to eat too.
Leave them be."

Slocum had the feeling that someone was riding on his trail.
He hoped that it was Morales and Bradley and not the Big O
bunch. Now and then he turned to look, but he saw no one
coming. He kept to his business, which was to track down
and catch Julia. Then he came across the grove of trees by the
stream where she had stopped. He looked it over and found
the tracks of a second horse. It seemed as if they had left together. He wondered who that could be with her. He let the

Appaloosa drink and graze a little. He was about to mount up and follow Julia and whoever she had fallen in with, when he saw the two riders coming. He waited in the trees. In another moment, he recognized Morales and Bradley. As they rode into the trees, he stepped out to reveal himself.

"Slocum," said Bradley in surprise.

"Holy shit," said Morales. "We thought you was dead in the storm."

"I imagine you searched real hard for me," Slocum said.

"Well . . ." Bradley began.

"Harman just took over," said Morales. "He said we should deliver the woman."

"So you all just rode on and left me there," said Slocum.

"Slocum," said Bradley, "we couldn't see you nowhere. We never seen your horse. We just figured that you went off in some other direction in the storm."

"Never mind all that," said Slocum. "It's in the past. How did Julia get away from you?"

Bradley and Morales both hung their heads. "We got drunk, I guess," said Morales.

"We thought she was getting drunk with us," Bradley added, "but I guess she tricked us."

"We passed out," Morales said, "and when we woke up, she was gone."

"Yeah," Slocum said. "I figured it was something like that. I stopped by that house and found you both still dead to the world."

"When we woke up," said Bradley, "we got on her trail first thing."

"Uh huh. What happened to Gil and Charlie?"

"They went into Bentley," said Bradley.

"What for?" Slocum asked.

Morales shrugged. "To have a little fun, I guess," he said.

"And they stayed gone all night?"

"I guess."

"Well, maybe they'll be coming along."

"I think maybe they will," Bradley said, "but I think they got some company."

"What are you talking about?"

"When we was fixing to ride out," Bradley said, "eight men come riding down on us. I think that two of them was Gil and Charlie. The others started in shooting, so we tuck off fast."

"Three of them come after us," said Morales, "but Bucky blowed them up sky high."

"Yeah," said Slocum. "Bucky's real good at that."

8

Davey Pool had wandered for several days before he wandered into the town of Lost Cause. Julia had finished tying her roll onto the back of her saddle, and he had told her to get mounted. She had, and when he turned to get on his own horse, she had whipped up her mount, knocked him down and slapped his horse. Pool fell over and his horse ran off. Julia was off like a shot. He had spent the better part of the rest of that day chasing down his horse and had completely lost Julia's trail. He was hungry and broke and dying for a drink of whiskey. His skin was chapped from the blistering desert sun, and he smelled like a wet polecat. The first thing he did was stop at the watering trough that stood in front of the Big Ace Saloon. He took off his hat and dunked his head in the water until he ran out of breath. Then he took a long drink. He filled his hat with water and poured it over his head. He left his horse drinking greedily at the trough, and walked into the saloon. He stood for a moment looking around. His mouth was watering for a drink, and he thought that he had made a bad mistake walking into the place. There was quite a crowd, and they were all drinking something. That just made Pool's pathetic condition seem all the worse.

"Something I can do for you, mister?" asked the bartender.

"Un, no," said Pool. "I was just looking for someone."

He turned to walk back outside, thinking that he might be able to sell his horse, maybe he could even get a day's work down at the stable. It wasn't exactly his style, but he was desperate. Then he heard someone call his name.

"Davey?" The voice said. "Davey Pool. That you?"

He turned back and saw a cowhand waving at him. He grinned when he recognized Abner Wickson, a puncher he had ridden with a couple of years back. He strode over to Wickson's table and shook hands. There were two other men at the table, and Wickson introduced them as Hardy Smythe and Bunch Cox. Then Wickson offered Pool a chair and a drink, and Pool sat down.

"It was some good luck running into you like this," Pool said. "I been wandering in that damn desert for days. Bunch I was riding with run me off by my lonesome in the middle of nowhere. I come into town here hungry and tired and broke."

"Oh, hell," said Wickson, "come on with me then. Boys, I'll be right back." He made sure everyone's glass was filled, then he took the bottle. He and Pool carried their glasses. Pool had no idea what Wickson was up to, but he let him lead the way. As they walked past the bartender, Wickson said, "Sammy, take another bottle over to my table, will you?" He tossed some coins on the bar.

"Sure 'nough," said Sammy.

"Come on, Davey," said Wickson. "I got a room upstairs." There was another man lounging at the far end of the bar, and when they came close to him, Wickson handed the man some money. "Send up a tub of hot water," he said. He led Pool up the stairs and into a room. Pool looked around. He finished his drink, and Wickson poured him another.

"You must be rolling in dough," he said.

"Ah, we done all right," Wickson said. "It ain't going to hold up forever though. But never mind that. You make yourself comfortable. I'm going back down to have you a meal fixed and sent up here. That tub'll be up here in a bit, and while you're taking care of all your worldly needs, I'll fetch you some new clothes. You got enough whiskey there, I think, for a little while."

"I'm doing just fine," said Pool. Wickson left the room. Pool sat down in the only chair in the room to sip his whiskey and consider his good fortune. "God damn," he said out loud. "It was high time."

Maxie and Slick were making their way slowly back toward Bentley. Slick was still woozy from the effect of the blast of dynamite that had blown him off his horse. He was weaving in the saddle. Maxie's broken leg hurt like hell. As they rode along, they passed a bottle back and forth.

"You think Olaf'll find that woman?" Slick asked.

"I don't know," said Maxie, "but if he does, I hope that gang ain't too big. There's just only three of them now since we got hurt."

"I ain't worried about Olaf in no fight," Slick said. "I'm just wondering if he does get that woman and takes her back to her husband and gets paid, will he give us our share?"

"By God, he better."

"He's like to say that we wasn't in on it and don't deserve no share."

"We was hurt being in on it. We deserve a share."

"I just hope that Olaf sees it that way."

"Well, he damn well better see it that way if he knows what's good for him."

Just then they made it down to the road and found themselves face to face with fifteen riders. They hauled back their reins and looked at each other. Then they looked at the riders. They had also stopped. No one said anything for a tense moment. Then one of the fifteen urged his horse forward. He rode up close to Maxie and Slick and touched the brim of his hat.

"Howdy," he said.

Both beat-up men responded, a bit nervously.

"You men live around here?"

"We live over in Bentley," said Maxie.

"My name's Loren O'Neill," said the man. "I run the Big O Ranch over west of here."

"I've heard of it," Maxie said.

"You got names?"

"Oh, yeah," said Maxie. "I'm Maxie and this here's Slick. You got to excuse my manners, Mr. O'Neill. I'm suffering from a bad broke leg. Slick here got his head knocked silly."

"What happened?"

"We was follering some men that had kidnapped a woman away from her husband, and one of the bastards throwed a dynamite stick at us. We're lucky to be alive, I guess, only right now it don't feel so lucky."

O'Neill worked hard at not letting his face show how he took that news. "Just the two of you?" he asked.

"No, there was six. There's three still trailing them."

O'Neill reached into his shirt pocket and pulled out a bill. "Why don't you tell me the whole story," he said.

Davey Pool was sitting in a tub of hot sudsy water. He had just finished a hot meal of steak and potatoes. He was puffing a cigar and holding a glass of whiskey. He could hardly believe how his luck had changed. Someone opened the door from the hallway, and Pool reached for his six-gun that was lying on a chair near the tub. The door opened, and a young, good-looking gal stepped in. She smiled. "Davey Pool?" she said, as she shut the door behind her.

"That's me," said Pool, putting the six-gun back down.

"Abner said that you might could use some company. They call me Amber."

"Well, Amber, baby," said Pool, "ole Abner knows what he's talking about sure enough,'cept only, I ain't got no cash."

"Don't worry about it, honey. Abner's took care of everything."

Amber started right in stripping off her clothes, and Pool's eyes opened wide. He put the cigar down in an ash-tray on the same chair with his six-gun, and he swilled down the rest of his drink, setting the glass down too. Amber stepped out of the last of her clothes and stood before him in all her resplendent and naked glory. She walked over close to the tub, and her lovely tits jiggled as she walked. Her ample hips swayed. She put a hand on Pool's head and ruffled his hair. "You want to get out," she asked, "or you want me to get in with you?"

"Come on in," said Pool.

Amber stepped high to get over into the tub, and as she did, Pool got his eyes full of what was there between her legs. As she settled down into the water, sloshing some over the edge of the tub, she spread her legs and wrapped them around his waist. She put her hands on his shoulders and pulled him close, giving him a long, deep, wet kiss. Pool felt his cock rising fast. He reached for her tits with both hands and squeezed them, her tongue still probing his mouth. Amber reached down between his legs and found the throbbing anxious tool.

"Oh," she said, looking down, "I do believe that you're raring to go."

"I ain't never been readier for nothing in my whole life," Pool said.

Amber raised her ass slightly and slid herself toward him, expertly guiding the ready rod into her damp and waiting slit. Pool reached around her, pulling her toward him and shoving himself more deeply into her. She humped back and forth, sending waves over the walls of the crowded tub. It didn't take long for Pool to spray forth, and he did so with a loud groan. Amber eased back off him and stood up. She looked down at him relaxing in the sudsy water. "Are you done, baby," she asked, "or you want to get dried off and get into bed?"

"I ain't done, Amber," he said. "Not by a long shot, I ain't."

Amber stepped out of the tub and picked up a towel. Pool was right behind her. She started drying him off, but he was impatient. He took the towel away from her and began rubbing her body all over. Soon, he said, "That's dry enough. Come on." He dragged her on over to the bed and threw her down on it. In an instant, he was on top of her, pumping away again.

As Maxie and Slick limped on toward Bentley, feeling a little better because of the money O'Neill had given them, O'Neill led his fifteen riders over the trail they had left behind them. "They're up ahead, boys," he called out as he rode. It didn't take long for them to reach the spot where Bradley and Morales had ambushed the Bentleyites. The first thing they saw was the bodies of the horses. Then they saw the remains of Harman and Case and the fresh burial site where Olaf Johnson had had his brother Sven laid to rest. O'Neill looked it all over carefully. Then, satisfied that the information he had paid for was valid, he led his men off again, this time following the trail left by Bradley and Morales and their three pursuers.

Callaway had been riding a short distance behind Jugs and Johnson, so he was the first to see the fifteen riders coming hard. He whipped up his horse and raced ahead to catch his two partners. "Olaf," he yelled as he approached. Johnson and Jugs halted their mounts.

"What is it?" Johnson said.

"There's fifteen riders coming hard on our tail," said Callaway.

"Fifteen?" said Johnson. "Who the hell could they be?"

"I don't know, but I seen them coming, and they're right on our trail."

Johnson thought hard for a moment. Then he climbed down out of his saddle. "Boys," he said, "we can't fight fifteen, and we can't outrun them forever. Come on down. We'll build us a little fire and make out like we're just minding our own business when they come along."

"Are you sure, Olaf?" Callaway said.

"Just climb down and relax and have faith in the Lord," said Johnson. "Above all, have faith."

•   •   •

When Abner Wickson thought that he'd given Pool ample time, he walked back up to the room. When he stepped in, Pool and Amber were still in bed and still naked, but they were drinking whiskey. "Oh," said Amber, pulling up a sheet in a vain attempt at modesty.

"Run along, Amber," Wickson said. Then he looked at Pool. "All right?"

"That's just fine," said Pool, slapping Amber on the bare ass as she crawled out of bed. She squealed and started grabbing up her clothes. While she was climbing into enough clothes to leave the room, Pool sat up on the edge of the bed and pulled on his new britches. He was feeling smug. He felt as if he had just about made up for losing out on that damned Hodges bitch, not once but twice. Wickson sat on the lone chair. Amber blew Pool a kiss and left the room. Pool took a slug of whiskey and looked at Wickson.

"What's this all about, Abner?" he asked.

"Just being friendly-like," Wickson said. "You looking for a catch of some kind?"

"I'm just wondering what you expect to get out of me," said Pool. "We've been friends for a spell, but I never knowed you to be quite this generous."

Wickson laughed. He took a cigar out of his pocket and offered it to Pool. Pool took it, and Wickson took out another and stuck it in his own mouth. Then he got a match and struck it on the bottom of the chair. He lit both smokes. "There ain't no catch, Davey," he said. "You can ride out of town and never owe me a dime for this. Just call it my hospitality." Pool looked suspiciously at Wickson. "You can if you want," Wickson continued. "But I would like to make you a proposition. I just figured you might be in a better mood to listen to me after all this."

"Okay," said Pool. "So here it comes. Well, all right, ole pard, I'm listening, but if I don't like it, I ride out and no hard feelings. Right?"

"That's right."

"Okay, shoot."

•   •   •

O'Neill came up on the three men sitting around a small fire with a coffeepot sitting nearby. Each man held a tin cup. Three saddles were on the ground, and three unsaddled horses grazed nearby. The fifteen riders all rode up close, stirring the dirt around and kicking up clouds of dust. Johnson looked up at O'Neill, who was clearly in the lead.

"Climb down and set a spell," he said. "You're welcome. We ain't got hardly enough to share with all of you, but you can rest yourselves at our camp, and you can make use of our fire if you have any coffee or anything you want to cook."

O'Neill dismounted, but the rest of his crew stayed in their saddles. "I'm Loren O'Neill," he said. "What's your names?"

"We're the Williams boys from up north, headed down toward Mexico," said Johnson.

"And you're a god damned liar," said O'Neill. "Your name is Olaf Johnson, and you're trailing a bunch of kidnappers. You mean to take the woman they stole and take her back to her husband to collect a ransom."

"Now, wait a minute," Johnson started, but O'Neill cut him off short.

"Shut up," he said. "I know all about you. You got two choices. You can do what I tell you, or we'll kill you where you sit."

"Wha—What do you want?" asked Johnson.

"Pull out your six-guns and toss them over here." The three unlucky men did as they were told. "Now pull off your boots and do the same with them."

They did that. O'Neill saw the rifles in the saddle boots. He told the three men to stand up and walk away from the saddles. They did, hobbling a bit as they walked over the rough ground in their bare feet. Olaf Johnson, being the oldest of the three, looked particularly pathetic.

"All right," said O'Neill, "three of you boys get down and saddle their horses. Stuff their guns and boots into their saddlebags."

Five cowhands dismounted, and three of them picked up

the saddles while the other two gathered the boots and guns. Soon the job was done.

"Now, Johnson," said O'Neill, "you three can come on back over here and sit down again by your fire. Drink your coffee."

He swung back up into his saddle. "Bring those horses, boys," he said, and he led his crew away again on the trail of Morales and Bradley. Johnson stood up by the fire and yelled at the top of his voice.

"Hey, you can't do this to us. We'll die out here with no horses and no guns. This is murder. Just plain damn murder. Come back. Come back here, you nasty son of a bitch." But his words were wasted, and soon the fifteen riders were out of sight. In another minute, he stopped staring after them and sat back down. "Pour me a cup of coffee," he said, holding out his tin cup. Jugs picked up the pot and poured the coffee. Johnson took a long sip. "Dirty son of a bitch," he said. "I'm going to kill that O'Neill. You mark my words. I mean to kill him deader'n a god damned squashed snail."

"I'll help you," said Callaway.

"Me too," said Jugs.

"I'd like to hang him," the old man said, "but I may have to settle with shooting him from ambush if he keeps that many men around him all the time."

"Who the hell is he?" asked Callaway.

"You recollect what them two we strung up told us? O'Neill's the fucker who first stoled the Hodges woman from her own husband. Now this other bunch has stoled her back, and O'Neill's after them."

"Oh."

"Well, what're we going to do, Olaf?" Jugs asked.

"We're going to set here and drink our coffee," Johnson said. "Then we're going after our horses and guns."

"In bare feet?" Callaway said.

"You want to set here and die?"

"Well, no, but—"

"Then don't argue with me. We're going to get them back. Then we're going to kill that O'Neill bastard, and then we're going to catch up that stole gal and take her back to her husband and collect the reward. How's that set?"

"That sets good, Olaf," said Callaway.

"I just wish we had our damn boots," said Jugs.

9

Slocum, Morales and Bradley found the place where Pool had come across Julia. It looked like someone had come across Julia and caught her. Slocum had no idea who it could be, but after studying the prints, Morales said, "Hey, looky here." Bradley and Slocum walked over to where Morales was on his knees. The Mexican pointed to a hoofprint. "I recognize this one," he said. Slocum looked and saw a distinctive print, a shoe with a slash across one side.

"Whose is it?" he said.

"It's Davey," said Morales. "Davey Pool. Remember?"

"Pool, huh?" Slocum said. "Yeah. I remember. So he's got Julia."

Morales crawled along the ground studying the marks he found there and looking for places where the grass was mashed down, where a twig was broken, anything out of the ordinary. "Yeah," he said, "he got her all right." He kept crawling and studying. "Hey, Slocum."

"What is it?"

"She climbed on her horse, and then she knocked Davey on his ass and rode away fast. Davey's horse ran away without no one on his back."

"Are you sure?" asked Slocum, hurrying over to the spot Morales was perusing.

"Look for yourself." Morales pointed out the more important features of the sign he had discovered. Slocum opined that he was reading them correctly. So Julia was once again out on her own, and now Davey Pool was somewhere wandering about. Slocum was glad he had busted Pool's knife, but he couldn't think of anything else about this mess to be glad of.

"All right," he said. "Let's mount up. We'll follow the woman's tracks, but keep your eyes peeled for any sign of Pool or of those Big O riders, or anyone else who might be out here wandering around the countryside."

Olaf Johnson had always fancied himself a tough old son of a bitch, but after walking for about a mile, searching for his horse and the other two, he began to think that he was a real tenderfoot. His feet were bruised, blistered, cut and bloody. Jugs and Callaway were just as bad off. Johnson felt as if he were barely moving, but the other two had fallen several paces behind him. Jugs was crying.

"Shut up that whimpering, you little chicken shit," said Callaway.

"My feet's ruint," sobbed Jugs. "I'll never be the same again. Not ever."

"Mine ain't no better off," Callaway said, "but you don't hear me bawling like a baby, do you? I'd be ashamed of myself to bawl like a baby. I'd be embarrassed to be acting like that in front of two growed men. I'm going to tell everyone in Bentley when we get back."

"You wouldn't do that," said Jugs. "Why would you do a thing like that?"

"Because you're such a god damned baby. That's why."

Johnson stepped on a sharp rock that took a slice out of the side of his right foot. He yelped and hopped on his left a couple of times, then fell over. He was holding his cut foot in both hands.

"What happened, Olaf?" said Callaway.

"I cut my foot off," Johnson said. "Ow. Damn it. Shit. Hell. Damn."

Jugs hobbled up close to get a better look. "Aw," he said, "it ain't near cut off."

"It's bleeding like hell," Johnson said.

"You walk on that," Callaway said, "you'll get dirt and shit all up in that cut, and you'll likely wind up getting it cut off for real or else die of something terrible."

Johnson untied the bandana from around his neck and tied it around his wounded foot like a bandage. That seemed like a good idea, so he pulled off his shirt and started ripping it into strips for the same purpose. Pretty soon Jugs and Callaway were sitting on the ground tearing their own shirts to shreds. When they were all done, Johnson got to his feet. He winced in pain, but he tried a few steps. His feet still hurt like the devil, but not nearly as much as they had before. "Let's go," he said.

"I can't walk no more," said Jugs. "I can't take another step."

"Well then, set there and die," Johnson said. "If I had my gun, I'd do you a favor and shoot you, but I ain't got it."

"We could beat him over the head with a rock," said Callaway.

"That'd take too damn long," said Johnson. "His god damn head's too hard. Come on. Leave him."

Johnson and Callaway started walking. They moved just a little faster than they had before they bound up their feet with rags. "Hey," said Jugs. "Hey. Don't leave me." He struggled to his feet and started hobbling along behind them, sobbing with each painful step.

Abner Wickson poured Davey Pool another glass of whiskey and handed it to him. Pool sat on the edge of the bed. Wickson sat on the lone chair. He poured himself a glass. Pool took a drink from his glass, eyeballing Wickson over the top edge of the glass. "I'm waiting," he said. "I'm waiting to find out how you expect to be paid back for all this nice stuff you been doing for me."

"Did you notice anything about this town when you come riding in?" said Wickson.

"Nothing in particular," said Pool. "It's just another town."

"Well, I noticed it right away," Wickson said. He paused to take a drink.

Pool waited. "Well," he said, "what?"

"It's got a bank, Davey. A nice little bank."

"Oh, shit. There can't be much money in this dipshit town. It wouldn't be worth the risk."

"In the first place, there wouldn't be that much of a risk. There's only one old lawman. He can't move very fast, and if we take it when it first opens up in the morning, there won't be that many folks out on the street."

"Okay, but like I said—"

"Davey," said Wickson. "Listen to me."

Pool shrugged. "I'm listening," he said, and he took another drink.

"There's a big mine west of here, and this here is the nearest bank to it. Once a month, they ship the payroll in here and keep it at the bank till the company sends out a crew to fetch it out to the mine. It's sometimes here two or three days before that happens."

Pool's eyes opened wider, and he leaned forward in his chair. "How much?" he said.

"I don't know," said Wickson. "I ain't never heard. But like I said, it's a big mining operation. It has to be a big payroll. You in?"

"Them two downstairs," said Pool. "Are they in on this?"

"Yep. They're good men."

"That'd be four of us."

"So you can count. Are you in?"

"Let's go out and look it over. You can tell me how you plan to do it."

Boone Conley had been leading the other bunch of Big O riders, the ones that Bucky Bradley had trapped behind his dynamite blast in the narrow valley. Not having any idea what had happened during the big storm, he had taken his bunch back west and out of the valley and then swung south.

Now he was leading them east, but he was way south of any of the rest of the parties involved. Further, he only knew of two other groups out there: the rest of the Big O riders with O'Neill, and the kidnappers they were pursuing. He was pissed off that he had been slowed down so much, but he was determined to get around the valley and back up north on the trail of the kidnappers and Julia. O'Neill might get her all right, but in case he did not, Conley meant to be there on the job.

Morales rode a little ahead of Slocum and Bradley. He was a damn good tracker, and Slocum knew it, so he had put the man out front. Morales halted his horse and dismounted. He knelt on the ground and studied some horse shit in the trail. Then he stood up and turned to face Slocum, who had ridden up close.

"She ain't far ahead now," he said. "I bet you when we top that rise up there, we'll see her."

"Okay," Slocum said, "let's ride."

While Morales was mounting his horse, Slocum moved out in front. He rode at a gallop, with Morales and Bradley coming up close behind him. Slocum was on top of the rise in a short while, and he reined in his Appaloosa and looked around. Morales and Bradley came up and stopped beside him.

"There," said Morales, pointing almost straight ahead. Slocum squinted and saw the horse and rider in the distance.

"Where the hell's she going?" he asked.

Morales shrugged. "Nowhere," he said. "I think she's lost."

"There ain't nothing out that way," said Bradley. "Not for miles."

"Let's go get her," Slocum said, and he whipped up his horse. The others followed. They rode at a gallop for a ways. Julia did not see them, and she was riding easy. They had closed about half the distance to her when she looked over her shoulder and saw them coming. She kicked her horse and lashed at it with the reins. "Come on," Slocum shouted. The Appaloosa outdistanced the other two horses easily. It was taking the open prairie with long easy strides, shortening the distance between itself and the other horse. Julia looked back again. She saw that it was Slocum and that he was getting closer. She lashed at her mount, desperate to escape. She thought that she could easily get away from the other two, but the Appaloosa was strong and fast.

Suddenly she shrieked as her horse stumbled and fell forward, throwing her over its head. She ducked her own head as she flew through the air and managed to roll when she hit the ground. She was sitting up, trying to clear her head when Slocum rode up and stopped beside her. Her horse struggled to its feet, seemingly unhurt by the mishap. Slocum dismounted.

"Are you hurt?" he asked.

"I don't think so," she said.

He gave her a hand up and she dusted herself off.

"Walk around a little," he said.

Morales and Bradley rode up then and halted their mounts. Julia took a few steps.

"I'm okay," she said. "My horse—"

"He seems to be all right too," said Slocum. "Morales, you want to check that animal over?"

Morales jumped down out of the saddle and walked over to the confused horse. He stroked it and talked to it, and then he walked it around some.

"He got shook up," he said, "but he's all right."

"Oh good," said Julia.

Slocum looked around for a good spot. Then he nodded toward a place on a slope. "We'll rest up for a spell over there," he said. "Morales, I think we can afford to have a little fire and some coffee."

"I'll gather up some wood," said Bradley.

"You might not find much," said Morales. "Look for some dry shit."

Slocum took Julia by the arm. They walked toward the knoll leading their horses.

"I don't blame you for trying to get away," he said, "but you sure as hell weren't headed for Pennsylvania."

10

Julia pouted at Slocum and the other two. When anyone came near her or said anything, she tossed her nose up in the air and spun around, turning her back on him. Morales got some coffee made and poured a round for everyone. Julia did take the coffee. Still, she didn't speak to anyone. After she finished her coffee, though, she walked over to the fire and held the cup toward Morales. "May I have some more?" she asked.

"Of course," Morales said, and he poured her cup full once more.

"Thank you," she said. She took a sip, then looked toward Slocum where he sat some distance away. She walked over and sat beside him.

"I guess I really am glad you caught up with me," she said.

"Oh, yeah?"

"I was hopelessly lost. At least I have a chance of staying alive with you. That is, until you turn me over to Asa." She glanced sideways at Slocum. His face wrinkled and he looked away from her. Good, she thought. He's feeling guilty. I may still have a chance with him.

Slocum was thinking that he did not want to hand Julia over to Hodges. He did not hold with brutality toward women. He would just as soon shoot any man who would treat a woman badly. But he had made a deal, and he always tried to keep his word. And Julia was Hodges's wife. He wasn't too worried anymore about the feeling of his companions. There seemed to be only two of them left, and he felt sure he could handle Morales and Bradley. His only immediate worries, that he knew of, were the Big O riders, and he had not seen a sign of them for some time now. But he couldn't figure out what to do about Hodges.

"Slocum," said Morales, "what are we going to do now?"

"We'll take the most direct route back to the ranch," Slocum said. Julia's face fell.

"What if we run into those Big O boys?" said Bradley.

"We'll just have to deal with that when the time comes," said Slocum. "They maybe gave up already and went back home," said Morales.

"Maybe," said Slocum.

"Don't count on it," said Julia. "Loren just might kill all three of you yet."

Three of O'Neill's riders were leading extra horses, the ones they had taken from Johnson, Jugs and Callaway. They had ridden some distance since abandoning the three wretches. O'Neill looked back over his shoulder to see the three riders with the extra encumbrance bringing up the rear. He halted his whole crew and waited for them. When they came up with the rest, he said, "Boys, I don't think those three are going to make any time at all what with the way we left them. If they do make any time, I expect it will be back toward Bentley."

The cowboys laughed, and one said, "Yeah, Boss. I don't think they want to tangle with us anymore."

"Turn those horses loose," O'Neill said. "We've brought them far enough."

Charles Tipton walked briskly down the street. It was early morning, and there were few people out. When he did encounter anyone, he politely tipped his bowler and said, "Good morning." He was nattily dressed in a three-piece suit. The bank would not open yet for a couple of hours, but Tipton always showed up early and used the extra time to catch up on his work. Reaching the bank, he took the keys out of his pocket and unlocked the door. A man stepped up beside him and smiled. Tipton looked at the man. He did not recognize him.

"Something I can do for you?" he asked.

"Just go on and open the door," the man said.

"If you have banking business," said Tipton, "you'll have to wait for two more hours. The bank is not open till then."

A second man stepped from around the corner of the building and moved up close on Tipton's other side. "You're going in," he said. "We'll just join you."

Tipton looked from one man to the other. "Is this a robbery?" he asked.

"Call it a withdrawal," said the first man. He grabbed the door handle and opened the door. The other man shoved Tipton inside. Both men followed him in.

On the other side of the street, Davey Pool stood with Cox. "They're in," said Cox. "Bring the horses around." He then hurried on across the street and stopped in front of the bank. He looked up and down the street to make sure no one was watching. Then he opened the door and stepped in.

"Latch that door," said Wickson. Cox latched it. He looked out the window and saw Pool moving out on the street with their horses. So far everything was going all right. Wickson and Smythe had their six-guns out and trained on the banker. Cox pulled out his own.

"Open that safe," said Wickson, "and hurry up about it. Don't give us no shit about time locks or anything like that either. You either open it right now, or we'll kill you."

Tipton knelt beside the big safe and worked the tumblers. Wickson and Smythe stood just behind him. Cox stayed at the door watching the street. In a minute, Tipton had the safe opened. Wickson grabbed him by a shoulder and shoved him to one side. He pulled a canvas bag out from under his coat and slapped it into Smythe's chest. "Get in there and clean it out," he said. Smythe stepped into the vault and started shoveling cash into the bag. "Don't take all day," Wickson said. He looked nervously from Smythe to Tipton and then to Cox standing at the door. In another minute or two, Smythe came back out of the vault, the canvas bag bulging.

"That's all of it," he said.

Wickson looked at the tellers' drawers along the back side of the counter. "Is there anything in them drawers?" he asked.

"All the money is put into the vault every evening at closing," Tipton said.

Wickson grabbed Tipton again and shoved him over to the open door of the vault. "What are you doing?" said Tipton. "Don't. I'll die in there." Wickson gave him a shove, and Tipton sprawled on the floor of the vault. As he scrambled back to his feet, Wickson slammed the door and then spun the lock. He turned toward the counter.

"Check them drawers just in case," he said. Smythe jerked open the drawers and threw them onto the floor. None of them contained any cash. "All right," said Wickson. "Let's get the hell out of here."

Cox unlatched the door and looked carefully out the window. "All clear," he said, and the three men walked out of the bank and across the street to where Pool was holding their horses. They mounted up and rode casually out of town, heading south.

Jugs was still whimpering with the pain and for his misfortune, and Callaway was still cursing him for it. Johnson stepped on the edge of a rock with the foot he had cut earlier, and even through the thick mass of rags tied around the foot, the pain shot up his leg and into his stomach. He yelled as he fell over. "You all right, Olaf?" said Callaway.

Johnson got himself into a sitting position. "Yeah. Hell yeah. Let's rest up here for a few minutes."

The other two squatted down on the ground facing Johnson. Jugs wiped at his eyes and sniffled. "Right now," said Callaway, "I wish we'd have brung that coffeepot with us."

"We'd have lost it way on back down the trail," Johnson said. "You know that."

"I know, but I still wish we had it."

"If wishes was horses then beggars would ride," said Johnson.

Jugs's sobbing had ceased, but his face still wore an expression of extreme pain, and he held his feet in his hands and rocked back and forth moaning low.

"Do you have to make all that noise?" Callaway said.

"I'm hurting here," said Jugs. "I'm hurting real bad."

"No more than the rest of us," said Callaway.

"Oh," moaned Jugs. "Oh, god damn. God damn."

"Shut up," said Callaway. "I wish I had my six-gun. I'd put you out of your fucking misery with just one little bullet."

Jugs looked directly at Callaway and grinned. "If wishes was horses," he began.

"Shut up," said Callaway.

"Olaf said it," protested Jugs.

"Both of you shut up," said Johnson. "I got to get me a little rest here."

"Olaf?" said Jugs. He was staring ahead with wide eyes.

"What?"

"He done told you to shut up," said Callaway.

"I don't care," said Jugs. "Look at what I'm a-looking at."

Both other men followed Jugs's eyes. Callaway rubbed his eyes with his fists. "Praise the Lord on high for his everlasting mercy," said Johnson. "I don't believe it's a mirage."

"Them's our horses," said Callaway.

"Our very own," said Jugs. "It's them. It's really them."

"Just set still and keep quiet," Johnson said. "Don't do nothing to spook them. We sure as hell can't go chasing them the shape we're in."

It took a few minutes, but the horses wandered in closer, and then Johnson started talking to them in a low and soothing voice. One of the horses looked up, nickered and shook his head. The other two continued grazing.

"Wish I had my rope," said Callaway.

"Wish I had my good feet," Jugs said.

"Now, you two just keep your voices calm and kind," said Johnson. "We'll talk them on over here."

"I was just thinking," said Jugs, "if we get holt of them horses, I don't know how I could get my swollen and wrapped up feet in the stirrups."

"Well," said Johnson, "me and Callaway will just mount

up on ours and then we'll chase yours off again if it's worrying you that much."

"No. Now, I wouldn't want you to do that, Olaf. I wouldn't want you leaving me stranded out here like that again."

One horse came in close, and Johnson got a hand on it. Pretty soon he was standing and stroking the animal's neck. At last he stuffed his foot into the stirrup and swung up into the saddle.

"Good for you, Olaf," said Jugs.

"Keep your voice calm," Johnson said. He turned the horse toward the nearest of the other two and rode slowly and carefully toward it. It sidestepped a couple of steps away from him. He stopped and talked and then moved toward it again. Soon he had its reins, and he led it back to Callaway, who stood up and took the reins.

"Fetch mine," said Jugs. "Fetch mine."

"I've a mind not to," said Johnson. "Just keep quiet."

He rode on out toward the third horse, which was a little farther back. In another minute, Callaway was mounting and riding out at such an angle that he would come up on the side of the remaining horse opposite Johnson. Jugs's mount proved to be a little more stubborn than the other two, but within fifteen or twenty minutes, they had it. They delivered it back to Jugs.

"Oh, thank you, boys," said Jugs. "Thank you, thank you, thank you."

"Well, mount up then," said Johnson, "and let's get moving."

"Which way?" said Jugs.

"We're going after them ole boys what done this to us," Johnson said. He was reaching into the saddlebags for his gunbelt.

"But there was a dozen or more of them," said Jugs.

Johnson stayed in the saddle. With his gunbelt strapped on, he unwrapped most of the rags from his feet and pulled on his boots. Callaway followed suit. "We got our rifles back now," Johnson said. "We can pick them off from a safe distance. One, two, three at a time. We'll get them, and round ourselves up a good herd of horses at the same time."

"We might even run across that little gal," said Callaway.

"I ain't forgot about her either," said Johnson. "Now, hurry it up. Time's a-wasting."

Jugs could see no alternative but to do as Johnson said, so he started trying to get a foot into a stirrup. "Oh. Oh," he was saying.

"Come on, Callaway," said Johnson. "He can catch up to us if he ever gets his lard ass into the god damned saddle."

"Wait for me," said Jugs. "Hey, wait up. Oh, shit."

But Johnson and Callaway were riding on ahead.

Jules Hoggard was surprised to find the front door of the bank unlocked. He usually arrived at work about an hour after Tipton, and he always found the door locked. He shrugged and opened the door. Stepping inside, he stopped and looked around. There was no sign of Tipton. He knew that there was something wrong. Not only did Tipton always go in and lock the door behind himself, but he would never leave the bank with the door unlocked. Hoggard walked on in and behind the counter, and he saw the teller's drawers on the floor. Something bad has happened here, he thought. He thought about the vault. If robbers had been there, they would have gotten into the vault, or tried to. They might have made Mr. Tipton open it for them. He hurried to the vault and worked the combination. When he pulled the door open, Tipton came staggering out, gasping for breath. He fell into Hoggard's arms.

"Mr. Tipton," said Hoggard. "Are you hurt?"

Tipton sucked in a couple more deep breaths. "No," he said. "I'm all right. Go get the sheriff. We've been robbed."

In a matter of minutes, old Sheriff Hardy had a dozen men gathered into a posse. He had descriptions of the four bank robbers from Tipton, and he was leading the posse south out of town. "Men," he shouted, "shoot first and ask questions later."

"We're rich, boys," said Wickson, as they rode along headed south toward the Mexican border. "Rich. Hell, I ain't never seen that much money before at one time."

"I ain't seen so much money in my whole life," said Cox.

"Will they get a posse after us?" Pool asked.

"Oh, I guess they will," said Wickson. "But it'll take old Hardy all damn day to do it. We'll be across the border by then."

"I can hardly wait to start in spending this money down in old Mexico," said Smythe. "Whiskey and women and women and whiskey."

"Whiskey and women," repeated Cox.

"And good food," said Wickson. "All we can eat and all we can drink."

"And all we can fuck," said Cox.

They all laughed thinking about the fun they would be having soon south of the border. They had slowed their horses to a canter. No one was worrying about a pursuit.

"I'm going to buy me a fancy new set of duds," said Wickson. "A black suit. Three-piece. A white shirt and a black tie and a flat-brimmed black hat. New shiny black boots. I'll be the slickest dude in Mexico."

"Reckon we ought to get us baths before we get new clothes?" asked Cox.

"Hell," said Wickson, "Davey's done had his bath, but I reckon maybe the rest of us could get us one before we put on our new duds."

Up ahead, Boone Conley halted his bunch of Big O riders and pointed at the four men riding toward them. "Reckon who that is," he said.

"They ain't got no woman with them," said one of the riders.

"They still could be part of that bunch," said Conley.

Just then, Pool saw the bunch of riders. "Posse," he shouted.

"How the hell did they get south of us?" said Wickson.

"Hell, I don't know," said Pool, "but there they are."

Cox panicked and pulled out his six-shooter. He fired a wasted shot toward the riders.

"That's got to be them," said Conley. "Let's ride."

11

The Big O riders cut loose with an incredible volley of shots from both rifles and pistols, and Cox shrieked, riddled with bullet holes. He fell from his horse with a thud, his body spurting blood from several different holes. Pool looked down in horror. "My God," he said.

"Come on," said Wickson. "Leave him."

"Should we separate?" said Smythe.

"With you carrying all that loot? Hell no," said Wickson. "Come on, damn it. Let's get out of here."

They headed in the opposite direction from the border, riding north for their lives, thinking that a big posse was in pursuit of them. Bullets were flying around them. As they rode, they turned in their saddles and fired wild shots at their pursuers.

"We're dead men," Smythe shouted.

"We ain't got a chance," said Pool.

"Shut up and ride," shouted Wickson.

They topped a rise with a grove of trees off to their left. No one gave a thought to riding into the trees. With such a large bunch after them, they would be trapped like rats. Their only chance was to outrun the chasers. They lashed their mounts. But suddenly they saw coming at them from the front a force nearly equal in size to the one behind them. They reined in their horses in a panic.

"Holy shit," said Pool.

"What the hell's that?" said Smythe.

"Make for the trees," said Wickson, and the three riders made a hard left turn and headed into the grove of trees. Conley would have followed them, but just as he was about to make that decision, he saw the other large bunch coming straight for him.

"Take cover, boys," he yelled. "They've got pardners."

The Big O riders dismounted and took whatever cover they could find—a lump in the earth, some tall grass; a few made their horses lie down on their sides and got behind them for cover. When Sheriff Hardy, leading the real posse after the bank robbers, saw the gang in front of him taking cover, he shouted similar orders, assuming that the robbers had an army of accomplices. The shooting started, and it sounded like a small war.

In the grove of trees nearby, Wickson, Smythe and Pool sat on their horses peering out in amazement. "What the hell's going on out there?" asked Smythe.

"I ain't got no idea," said Wickson, "but whatever the hell it is, it just saved our ass. Let's ride out of here the back way. Say, how does Montana sound to you fellas?"

They picked their way through the woods and started riding north, leaving the war to rage behind them.

It had taken Jugs quite some time to get into the saddle. He found that he could barely stand, and when he got hold of his horse's saddle and tried to get a foot into the stirrup, the foot was wrapped so thick that he couldn't poke it in. He cried and whined, talking to the horse, begging it to stand still. Johnson and Callaway were already out of sight. At last, he managed to drag his upper body across the saddle. He struggled for several minutes before he could get his leg over and finally actually sit in the saddle. He left both feet dangling. Left alone, he was in too big a hurry to do as the others had done, unwrapping their poor feet and pulling on their boots. He had to catch up with them. He did not want to be left alone out in the middle of nowhere with God knows who riding around with all kinds of mischief on their minds.

Jugs had a low tolerance for pain. As he rode along, he moaned and sobbed out loud. As his loose hanging feet bobbed up and down with the horse's gait, pain shot up through his legs and into his gut, making him want to scream. For a while he thought about turning around and heading back toward Bentley, but he looked over his shoulder, and he wasn't sure that he could find the way by himself. He did think he could catch up with Johnson and Callaway, so he kept on their trail, but a nice easy chair back in Bentley and a pan of hot water on the floor for his wretched feet sure did seem like a grand idea. He tried to ride fast, but when he did, the pain was just worse. He held his horse at a gallop.

Asa Hodges was pacing on his front porch, looking off in the direction from which Slocum and his gang would come riding in. It had been too long. Slocum should have returned with Julia days ago. Something had gone wrong. Suddenly Asa stopped pacing, took the big cigar out of his mouth and threw it down hard on the porch. He shouted at the top of his lungs for his foreman, Simp Culley. In a couple of minutes, Culley came running up to the porch. "You call me, Boss?" he asked.

"Saddle my horse, Simp," Hodges said, "and round up about six or so of the best boys with guns. Bring them over here to the house right away."

"Yes, sir." Culley ran off to do as he'd been told, and Hodges went back into the house. He got his six-gun and belt and strapped them on around his waist. Then he put on his jacket and hat and went back outside to wait. It wasn't long before Culley and six other riders came up to the porch. Culley was leading Hodges's saddled horse. Hodges went down from the porch and mounted up. He turned the horse toward the gate that would lead him off the ranch and then on out west, and started to ride. The seven cowhands followed him. None of them knew where they were going or what they might be in for. They followed Hodges blindly.

O'Neill and his riders found a spot beside a stream where they could stop and rest and water their horses. They built a small fire and made some coffee. Then O'Neill decided that they could take the time to fix a meal. The horses either drank at the stream or grazed along its bank. Across from the stream was a bluff. O'Neill sat down beneath a large tree to drink a cup of coffee.

Up on the bluff, Johnson and Callaway crept close to the edge. They snuggled down in some tall grass that grew right up to the edge of the bluff. "That's them all right," Callaway said.

"The very ones," said Johnson. "Retribution has come, praise the Lord."

"Olaf," said Callaway. "There's more than a dozen of them. I count fifteen, I think. The two of us can't fight fifteen men."

"We'd just only have to shoot seven or eight of them each is all," said Johnson. "Can't you shoot seven men from such a good spot as this?"

"Well, maybe," said Callaway. "But likely, we'd get four or five of them, and the rest would start in shooting back and moving in on us."

"They can't climb this bluff," said Johnson. "We got them right where we want them, thanks to the Lord."

"I don't know, Olaf. I just ain't real sure."

"We'll wait a few minutes," Johnson said. "It looks to me like they're fixing to eat. Let's let them get real involved in their meal, and then we'll cut loose on them."

Slocum rode beside Julia, with Morales and Bradley riding behind them. They were headed for Hodges's ranch. They rode along in silence, Slocum deep in thought. He had noticed that Julia was a good-looking woman, but only now was he thinking about what it would be like to bed her. She was damn desirable, but the thought was tormenting, because it led to thoughts about what would happen to her when she was returned to her husband. He reviewed in his mind all kinds of possible scenes to follow. He thought about just riding off with her, spending a few nights and then sending her on her way to Pennsylvania. But he had made a deal, and he hated the thought of going back on his word once it had been given. Then too, he might have to fight Morales and Bradley if he failed to get the money from Hodges.

He considered delivering her to her husband, collecting the money and then killing the son of a bitch. That wasn't a bad thought, but there were drawbacks there too. Maybe Hodges would refuse to fight. Could Slocum shoot the man down in cold blood? And what about all the ranch hands who might be hanging around? Could he fight them all off? If he were to kill Hodges, Julia would be safe, but did he really want to sacrifice himself for her safety? He didn't think so. The only way he would want to save her was if he could save himself at the same time. And then, even if he did manage to kill Hodges and get away from the ranch with Julia, the Big O riders might well still be on their trail. He wasn't sure they would ride all the way into Hodges's ranch after Julia, but they might. Slocum tried to think if he had ever been in such a tight spot, but nothing came to mind.

O'Neill and his men all had plates of food and were settled down to eat, when Johnson heard hoofbeats coming up behind him. He tapped Callaway on the shoulder. "It's only just one horse," he said. "Slip back there and check it out." Callaway eased backward through the tall grass until he was near where they had left their horses. He stayed low until the rider came into view. Then he recognized Jugs. Jugs recognized the horses. He pulled up beside them and looked around.

"Olaf?" he said.

Callaway came out of hiding. "Keep quiet," he said.

"Oh, there you are. Where's Olaf?"

"Hush up, I tell you. Get down off that horse."

"I can't get on my feet no more," Jugs said. "They're hurting something fierce."

"You ain't getting on your feet. You're getting on your belly, and we're crawling up yonder." He gestured toward the lip of the ledge behind him. "Come on now."

Jugs still did not move. "What's going on?" he asked.

"Olaf is up there watching that bunch that done this to us," said Callaway. "Now, get down, and bring your rifle."

Jugs struggled to get off his horse, and even though Callaway had told him that he was not going to be on his feet, he had to light in a standing position. He winced, and his knees buckled, but he held on to the saddle horn and, whimpering the whole time, pulled the rifle from the saddle boot. Then he dropped to his knees. He crawled alongside Callaway until they were back where Callaway had left Johnson.

"So you made it, did you?" Johnson whispered to Jugs.

Jugs looked at the scene below. "What are you planning to do?" he said.

"We're going to kill them all," said Johnson. "Now that you're here with us, we'll only have to shoot five men each. Get ready."

"Hold on," said Jugs. "I'm hurt bad enough already. The odds is just too great against us. That man will do us worse if he gets hold of us a second time. Hell, he might strip us nekkid or something."

"You in pain, Jugs?" said Olaf. "Your feet swole up and bleeding? You can't even stand up on them?"

"That's right," said Jugs. "I can't."

"Well, right down there is the man what done that to you. He done it to all of us. Now is our chance to get even with the dirty bastard. The Lord has give us this chance. Praise the Lord. Do you want to ignore a gift that the Lord has laid out before you?"

"Well, no, but—"

"Then chamber up a bullet in that rifle. You start shooting to your right. Callaway, you start to the left. I'll take them right square in the middle. Don't stop shooting till they're all dead."

Hodges rode until he decided that the horses needed a rest. He called a halt, and he gathered his men around him. "We'll rest up the horses a bit," he said. "Now, I think it's about time I let you know what we're up against, as much as I can. You all know that I sent out Slocum and six men to bring my wife back home safe from the Big O Ranch. She was kidnapped by Loren O'Neill. I thought if anyone could do it, it would be Slocum. He's some kind of gunfighter. I could tell by watching him. But he's been gone too long. Something's happened. Could be that O'Neill got them, and Julia's still there at the Big O. Could be that Slocum got her away, and the Big O boys is after them. Could be that Slocum got her and has run off with her himself. Anything could have happened, and we have got to be ready for whatever we run into. The main thing is I want her back safe. Now, if any of you don't want to get in on this thing, now's the time to let me know. I won't hold it against you."

There was a moment of silence before one cowhand stepped forward. "Speaking for myself, Boss," he said, "I'm sticking with you."

"Me too," said another one. "I always say, when you hire on with a man, you stand by him."

The rest all nodded in agreement and answered in the affirmative.

"I thought that would be your answer," said Hodges. "Now, let's all get mounted up again and get back on the trail."

A tremendous amount of ammunition had been expended by Boone Conley and his riders on the one side and Sheriff Hardy and his posse on the other, and no one had been hit. A man called Red was lying down close to Conley. "Say, Boone," he said. "Do you think there was that many men with them kidnappers?"

"I didn't think so," Conley answered.

"Well, just who the hell are we fighting then?"

The shots had slowed down to one every now and then. Conley shoved bullets into his Winchester. "Maybe we had ought to find out," he said.

Over on the other side, a posse member slithered over close to Sheriff Hardy. "Sheriff," he said, "I didn't think there was so damn many of them bank robbers."

"I thought there were just four," Hardy said.

"We're fighting a damned army over there," said the man.

"You're right."

"Hey, Sheriff, look." The man pointed across the way.

Hardy looked and saw a white flag raised on the end of a rifle barrel. "They're giving up."

"Or they want to talk," said Hardy. "Keep me covered." Slowly he stood up, holding his arms out to his sides. "What do you want?" he called out.

"I want to talk to you," Conley yelled from the other side.

"Walk on out," said Hardy. "I'll meet you halfway."

Conley stood up. "You men all hold your fire," he said. He started walking slowly toward Hardy.

Hardy looked to his right and then to his left. "No shooting now," he said. The prairie was suddenly deathly quiet as the two men walked slowly toward each other. All men on both sides held their weapons ready just in case something went wrong. When the men got close to each other, Conley squinted at the badge on the sheriff's vest.

"You a lawman?" he asked.

"I'm Sheriff Hardy of Lost Cause," Hardy said. "I'm leading a posse after some bank robbers. Who are you?"

"Boone Conley from the Big O Ranch. We're chasing some kidnappers."

"It appears that we got us a bad case of mistaken identity on both sides."

"I'd say so. Just before we come onto you, we seen four men in the road. They shot at us, and we shot back. We killed one of them. We was following them when you come along."

"That must have been the robbers," Hardy said. "Do you know where they went?"

"No. Whenever you come down the road, you took all our attention."

"Where's the dead one?"

"Back down the road. I can show you."

"All right, but first let's let all our boys know that we ain't at war with one another."

"Yeah. Anyone hurt on your side?"

"No, sir."

"Ours neither. I reckon we're lucky at that. It could have been a whole lot worse."

12

When Boone Conley led Sheriff Hardy and the posse back to the body of Cox, one of the men recognized it. "He was hanging around Lost Cause for the last few days with a man called Wickson and another fellow. Let's see. I think his name was Smythe," he said.

"That's right," said another. "I knowed they was no good."

"Say," said yet another, "they picked up one more character. I never heard his name."

"So we're still hunting for three robbers and the money," said Hardy.

"Looks that way," said the man who had spoken first.

"Well," Conley said, "their trail led off kind of northwest, mostly north. If you don't mind, on account of we was shooting at you and held you up for a bit there, we'll ride along and help you hunt them. We might could run onto what we're looking for along the way."

"That's just fine with me," said Hardy. "Let's get going."

Olaf Johnson squinted his eyes and tried like hell to make out Loren O'Neill in the bunch down below, but O'Neill was sitting beneath a large tree and was hidden in the shadows. Johnson had to give it up. If he wanted to start shooting, he would have to pick another target for his first shot. He

103

moved his rifle around until he had an easy one. "All right, boys," he said, "commence to killing." He pulled the trigger, and a man sitting on the ground with a plate gave a jerk and fell backward. Callaway's shot knocked down a man who was leaning against a tree, and Jugs took a man in the back who was walking toward the horses. But as soon as the first shot sounded, the rest of the men dropped plates and cups, pulled out six-guns or ran for rifles, and took cover right quick. Three men were down but not another could be seen.

"God damn it, Olaf," said Jugs, "you said we'd take five each with no problem. Now we're really in for it. Now they know we're up here."

"Shut up, Jugs," said Johnson. "You should've shot faster."

"Well, how many did you get? Huh? You only got one, didn't you? I see three bodies down there, and I don't see no one else. There's still thirteen or fourteen of them, and they know we're here. Now they're going to kill us all. Sure as hell. They'll kill us all."

"I told you to shut up," said Johnson. "Just keep watching. Someone'll make a move, and we can get him."

Down below someone ran from behind one tree over to another, and Callaway fired a quick shot, but it only kicked up dirt.

"Damn," he said.

"Don't waste shells," said Johnson. "Waste not, want not."

"I thought I had him," said Callaway.

"Where the hell are those shots coming from?" O'Neill said.

Riley, his top hand, was nearby, and he answered, "I ain't sure, Boss, but I think they're coming from up on top of that ledge somewhere."

O'Neill scanned the ledge. It was a long stretch. They could be anywhere along that space. "We got to find out," he said.

"I'll find out," said Riley. "You all watch the ledge real careful. If anyone shows himself, shoot him."

"What're you going to do?" said O'Neill.

"Don't watch me," Riley said. "Watch the ledge." Then he took off running, showing himself for a target, and when he did, Callaway popped up beside a scrawny dead tree up on the ledge, leveled his rifle and fired. His bullet took Riley in the left thigh, and Riley yelped and hopped over behind a tree. O'Neill and several others fired in response.

Callaway screamed. One bullet tore off his thumb where it was lapped over the top of his rifle right near his nose. It also creased his nose, and it dented the rifle up above the lever. Callaway dropped the rifle over the edge of the rim. Blood ran down his face, but it looked much worse than it really was. His thumb was gone though. "Oh, shit," he said. "Oh, hell. I'm hit bad."

"You damn fool," said Johnson. "You fell for it."

"You got to stop the bleeding," Callaway said. "I could bleed to death here."

"Damn," said Jugs. "Your thumb's plumb shot off."

"Well, wrap your bandana around it," said Johnson. "We can't stop what we're doing now."

"I can't see. I got blood in my eyes."

"Oh, here," said Jugs, reaching over to undo the bandana from around Callaway's neck. He stuffed the rag into Callaway's hand. "Now wrap it up," he said. "And who's crying now?"

"Oh," Callaway moaned, wrapping his wounded hand up the best he could. "Oh, son of a bitch. God damn. Fuck."

"Stop that god damned cussing," said Johnson. "And keep quiet. You're distracting me from my good work."

Suddenly more shots hit the rim around them, and the three men ducked down low.

"He fell for it, all right," said Jugs. "Now they've got us located. Now they'll kill us for sure."

"No, they won't," said Johnson. "Scoot back'ards on your bellies to the horses. They can't see us back that far. Come on."

They worked their way back like inchworms while shots

still kicked up dirt in front of them on the rim. Pretty soon, they made it to the horses. Johnson got mounted in good time, but Jugs still cried when he stood up on his feet, and Callaway had trouble mounting up with only one hand and with his blurry eyes. They rode a little ways down from where they had been, and Johnson said, "Jugs, get off here."

"And what?" Jugs said.

"Get back up there on that ledge like we was before and get to shooting."

Jugs moaned out loud, but he dismounted and fell on his belly and started to crawl. Johnson and Callaway rode a little farther.

"I don't know what good you're going to do with no rifle and no thumb, but get off here and do what you can with your six-gun."

"I can't do nothing, Olaf," said Callaway. "It's my right thumb, and them shots is too far for a six-gun anyhow."

"Just get off and shoot. Make some noise," said Johnson. He rode down farther and dismounted, squiggling his way to the rim. Then he readied his rifle and looked for a target again.

While Johnson and the others had been busy relocating, Riley had taken two men and ridden fast to the far end of the rimrocks. They made their way around to the back side and rode cautiously, watching the ledge, which was now in front of them. Soon they spotted the gnarled tree where the three men had first been hiding, but no one was there. They rode on. In just a little while, they saw Jugs's horse. "They've spread out," Riley said. "Let's try to take him without shooting." They dismounted and sneaked up on Jugs. They took out their revolvers. "Lay down your rifle," said Riley, "and roll over on your back."

"Oh," said Jugs. "Don't shoot me. I told Olaf this was a bad idea." He put the rifle down and rolled over. "I really did. I told him we hadn't ought to bother you folks."

"Hey," Riley said. "This is one of those three we left barefoot. You must be slow learners."

"It was Olaf," said Jugs.

"Tie him up," Riley said.

"What are you going to do with me this time?" whined Jugs. "You ain't going to just leave me here?"

"I think we'll throw you over the edge," Riley said.

"Oh, no. Don't do that. Please."

"How many of you are up here?" Riley said.

"There's just three of us is all," answered Jugs. "Just three."

"Just three of you attacked fifteen men?"

"Olaf said we could easy get five apiece."

"Where are the other two?"

Jugs nodded his head to one side. "Down yonder way," he said. The cowboys had finished tying Jugs's hands and feet, and Riley nodded toward their horses.

"Let's go get the others," he said. They mounted up and rode on down the line till they spotted another horse. Again they dismounted and moved quietly up behind Callaway, who was just sitting and sniveling. He never heard their approach. "Just lay there on your belly," said Riley. "Don't move or you're dead."

Callaway did not move. The cowboys moved in close behind him and pulled his hands behind his back. He shrieked in pain. "Well, looky here," said one of the hands. "Someone shot off his thumb." They tied his hands behind his back.

"Stay here and keep quiet," said Riley. He motioned for the cowboys to follow him. They mounted up again and rode on to the next horse. They heard a shot fired up on the rim. "This is the last one," Riley said. "He's the ringleader too. Spread out and be careful."

Johnson fired another shot. He had not heard any shots fired from either Jugs or Callaway, and he wondered what the hell was wrong with them. Just wait, he thought, till I get them alone when this is over. I'll hit their damn feet with my rifle butt. That's what I'll do. He aimed and fired again. He cranked the lever and pulled the trigger. A click. His rifle was empty. "Damn," he said, and he rolled over to one side, reaching for more bullets in his belt. He saw a cowboy coming toward him. He dropped the rifle and went for the six-gun at his side, but a voice came from his other side.

"I wouldn't try it, mister."

He looked in that direction and saw two more. All three had their guns out and pointed at him. He rolled onto his back, laying his arms out at his sides.

"I guess you got me, boys," he said.

In another few minutes, Riley and the cowhands rode back into the camp below, leading three other horses with the trussed up captives on their backs. "Hey, Boss," Riley called out. "You'd never guess who we got here."

O'Neill stepped out from behind a tree. The rest of the hands all came out to see. "Just three of them?" said O'Neill. Then he recognized the three. "Well, I'll be damned."

"You will be too," said Johnson, "for a black sinner. You see what you've already done to us. You've ruint our feet, and now you've shot poor Callaway in the face and tuck off his thumb as well."

"You should've gone back where you came from," said O'Neill. "Now you've killed three of my men."

"They only got what they deserved," said Johnson. "I wish we'd a killed ever' last one of you. I'd a got you first off, but I couldn't catch sight of you."

"It was all Olaf," said Jugs. "Olaf done it all."

"Shut up, you sniveling coward," Johnson said. "I just wish I could get my hands on you two turn-coaty bastards."

"What'll we do with them, Boss?" Riley asked.

"What do you think?"

"String them up," someone shouted.

"They're killers," shouted another.

"Well then," said O'Neill, "get the ropes ready."

"No," said Jugs.

"You can't do that," said Callaway. "We deserve a fair trial. You've already shot off my thumb."

"It won't hurt much longer," said O'Neill.

Three cowboys secured ropes up over a long, stout tree branch, and three more moved the horses with the culprits on their backs under the branch. A cowboy on horseback rode over and slipped the nooses over the heads of the three wretches. Jugs and Callaway both whimpered, and Johnson growled.

"You got anything you want to say?" O'Neill asked.

"Don't do it, mister," said Callaway. "Please don't do it."

"I don't want to die," Jugs whimpered.

"Vengeance is mine, sayeth the Lord," Johnson shouted.

"Shall I spook the horses, Boss?" Riley asked.

"Wait a minute," said O'Neill. He walked over to stand in front of the three horses and looked up at the three men with nooses around their necks. "You think you can control those horses?" he asked.

"What?" said Jugs.

"What do you mean?" asked Callaway.

"I mean just like you are, tied up and all, can you control your horses?"

"What the hell are you talking about?" said Johnson.

"You said vengeance is the Lord's," O'Neill said. "Well, let's just find out how interested he is in what's going on down here. Mount up, boys."

"What are you doing, Boss?" asked Riley.

"Bring my horse over," O'Neill said.

All the cowboys mounted up and someone brought O'Neill's horse. He climbed into the saddle. "I ain't going to hang you," he said.

"Oh, thank you," said Jugs. "You're a good man. I'm sorry I shot at you. Truly I am."

"No," said O'Neill. "I ain't going to hang you. I'm just going to ride off and leave you like you are."

"What?" said Callaway.

"I'm going to leave it up to the Lord," Riley said. "If he wants to save you, he'll make sure those horses stand still, and he'll find a way to untie your hands. Good luck to you now."

He turned his horse and rode away. All the cowboys followed him. Johnson screamed curses at him. Jugs said, "Olaf, don't yell so loud. You'll spook the horses."

"You heathenish god damn son of a bitch," Johnson shouted, and his horse nickered and took a lurch forward, tightening the noose around Johnson's neck. Suddenly the value of Jugs's advice came home to him. "Whoa," he said softly. "Take it easy there, ole horse. Just calm down. Take it easy now. I wasn't yelling at you. No way."

"What're we going to do, Olaf?" Jugs said.

"What choice do we have, you ninny?" Johnson answered. "We're going to sit here till someone comes by to save our holy ass or else we starve to death or else our horses gets tired of holding still and walks out from under us."

"Can't you work your hands loose?"

"Shit holy fire," said Johnson. "I'm trussed up better'n a calf fixed for branding. How about you?"

"I'm tied pretty damn tight," said Jugs. "Callaway?"

"Even if I wasn't tied tight," Callaway said, "there ain't nothing I could do with my thumb shot off like it is. My whole arm hurts from it, and I'm sure to bleed to death sitting here."

"What was that bastard's name again?" said Johnson.

"Which one?" Jugs asked.

"The unholy son of a bitch what done this to us," said Johnson. "Who else?"

"Oh. That was O'Neill. O'Neill of the Big O Ranch."

"I'm going to remember that," Johnson said.

"It won't do you no good if we die setting here."

"I'm hurting all over, and I'm bleeding to death," said Callaway. "Hanging's better than that." He let out a ferocious scream and kicked his horse in the sides. The animal neighed and jumped forward, out from under Callaway, and Callaway swung in the breeze. The other two horses were startled by the suddenness and began to fidget, but Johnson and Jugs talked to them and managed to calm them down. Jugs turned his head slightly to look at the body swaying in the breeze.

"Olaf?"

"Yeah?"

"It's spooky setting here like this right next to a dead man what just hanged hisself."

13

Maxie and Slick sat in the saloon in Bentley. Maxie's leg had been tended to with a little more care than before. It had been set and wrapped tightly against a piece of board. He sat at a table with his leg propped up on a chair. A glass of whiskey sat on the table in front of him. Slick sat across from him at the same table. His head had mostly cleared up, but he still had a ringing in his ears. He too had a glass of whiskey. The bottle was on the table between them.

"How's your leg doing, Maxie?" Slick asked. "Is it still a-hurting you?"

"It's numbed down somewhat," said Maxie. "How about your head?"

"My ears is still ringing, but I just about got used to that, I reckon."

"Maxie, do you think that Olaf will share that money with us?"

"Not unless we kill him first."

Maxie picked up his glass and drained it. Slick did the same. Then he reached for the bottle and refilled both glasses. Mac was busy wiping down the bar. No one else was in the saloon. Outside the wind was blowing. It muffled the sound of the four horses that came up in front of the saloon. The front door opened, and a man stepped in, a whiff of dust coming in with him. He was followed by another man and then by a

111

woman. Finally, a third man came in behind and shut the door. He took off his hat and dusted it against his leg. The newcomers stood for a moment looking the place over.

"Howdy, strangers," said Mac. "Anything I can do for you?"

Slocum walked to the bar. "Can we get something to eat in here?" he asked.

"Got a pot of stew on," said Mac.

"We'll take it," Slocum said, "and a bottle of good sipping whiskey while we wait."

Mac brought out a bottle and four glasses, and Slocum took them to a table. Bradley, Morales and Julia followed him and sat down. He poured four glasses and passed them around. Then he took his first sip. It was good. Morales gulped his down all at once and pushed his empty glass toward Slocum. Slocum gave him a look and then refilled the glass.

"Slow it down, Esteban," he said. "I don't want you drunk as a skunk again."

"All right," said Morales, and he picked up his glass and took a tiny sip. "Is that better?"

"It'll do."

Mac came over to the table with four bowls of stew, four spoons and a loaf of bread on a tray. He put a bowl and spoon in front of each person and the bread in the center of the table. Then he went back to the bar. Across the room, Maxie and Slick were watching the newcomers with suspicious expressions on their faces. Slick got up and moved to a chair closer to Maxie. He leaned over so he could speak in a whisper into Maxie's ear.

"You reckon that's them kidnappers and the woman?" he said.

"I just bet it is," said Maxie.

"We could take her for ourselves and get all the money."

"How would we do that?" Maxie said. "There's three of them and two of us, and I've got a broke leg."

"Let's think on it awhile," said Slick. He poured more whiskey into both glasses.

Slocum tore a piece of bread off of the loaf. He dipped his

spoon into the stew and took a big bite. It was hot, and it was surprisingly good. The others were eating as well. While Slocum ate, he watched Slick and Maxie. He did not know them, but he did not like their looks, and the way things had been going, he did not intend to take any chances. He had carefully positioned himself at the table so he was facing them. The two tables were clear across the room from each other.

"We could just start shooting and kill them all before they know what's going on," Slick whispered into Maxie's ear.

"We might hit the woman," said Maxie, "and no one's going to pay to get his woman back dead."

Slocum noticed the two men sitting close and talking low, and he also took note of the fact that they were looking in his direction. Of course, they might just be suspicious of strangers in this jerkwater place. Now that he had seen it, he was surprised that it even had a name. There was nothing to it but the saloon. It did have a store attached, and it had rooms upstairs, but it was the only building in Bentley. Morales was sopping his bowl with a piece of bread, and Slocum finished his. He waved at Mac.

"How about four more bowls of stew," he called out. Mac brought out the pot and ladled out stew for each bowl. Then he went back behind the bar again. Slocum glanced at Julia. "You're being awful quiet," he said.

"You want me to carry on a casual conversation with my captors?" she said. "Friendly chatter? I don't feel casual or friendly."

Slocum heard the sound of a door shutting upstairs. He looked up at the landing and saw a woman heading down the stairs. She looked down at the newcomers and smiled, and she did her best to descend the stairs like a goddess. When she arrived at the bottom, she swayed her way over to the bar, then leaned across it to speak to Mac.

"You know these?" she asked him.

Mac shook his head. "They've never been in here before," he said.

"Have they got money?" she asked, thinking about her last experience with two strange cowhands.

Mac shrugged. "They ain't paid me yet," he said.

"Well," she said, "maybe I'll just check them out."

She ambled across the room and stopped just behind Slocum. "Hi, cowboy," she said. "They call me Sugar Tits."

"Pull up a chair and have a drink," Slocum said. "But I ain't interested in nothing else."

Sugar Tits turned and made a gesture toward Mac. Then she dragged a chair between Morales and Bradley. Mac got a glass and brought it over to her. She shoved it toward Slocum, who poured her a drink. "Thanks," she said. "I see you've already got a woman, so I'll just sit over here with these two big boys."

"I'm not his woman," said Julia.

"Oh," said Sugar Tits. "My mistake. Which one then?"

"I don't belong to any man," Julia said, "and especially not to any of these range tramps."

Across the room, Slick's ears pricked up. He whispered to Maxie, "Did you hear that?"

"I heard it."

"She's got to be the one."

"So what do we do?"

"Just wait and watch," said Slick, "for now."

"You boys got any money?" Sugar Tits asked. She was looking into the face of Bucky Bradley.

"I got a little," Bradley said.

"You want to go upstairs for a little nooky?"

Bradley looked over at Slocum. "You're a grown man," Slocum said. "Do what you want."

Bradley grinned wide and stood up, taking Sugar Tits by the arm. She stood up, and the two of them walked together across the room and up the stairs.

"There's just two now," Slick whispered.

Hodges, Culley and the others were riding west, searching for any sign of Slocum or of Julia. So far they had not had any luck. Culley urged his mount up beside that of Hodges. "Mr. Hodges," he said, "do you think it's about time for a rest?"

"You're right, Culley," Hodges said. "We'll slow down,

and you look for a suitable spot. Stop us when you see one."

They'd ridden on for about another mile when Culley spotted a tree line. "There must be a creek over there," he said. "Let's head for it."

They rode to the tree line, and sure enough, there was a small stream, running clear, clean water. They stopped and unsaddled their horses, allowing them to drink and to graze. A couple of the hands built a small fire and another boiled some coffee over it. Soon they were relaxed and drinking coffee. Hodges, though, did not relax. He was pacing nervously.

"Mr. Hodges," said Culley, "there's three riders coming this way."

Hodges and Culley stood side by side watching the coming visitors. In another couple of minutes, Pool, Smythe and Wickson rode up. They stopped their horses just in front of Hodges and Culley. "Howdy," said Wickson with a broad smile. "Could you folks stand a little company at your fire?"

"Get down," said Hodges. "There's coffee over there. Help yourselves." He was gruff and abrupt, bordering on rude, but he did offer the traditional range hospitality.

"If you want to unsaddle your horses," said Culley, "there's water and grass over there."

"Thanks," said Wickson. The three riders dismounted and started leading their horses toward where the others already grazed. When they'd gotten a distance away from Culley and Hodges, Pool put a hand on Wickson's shoulder.

"You know who that old man is?" he asked.

"Never saw him before. Why?"

"That's Asa Hodges. The man I told you about. The one who sent me and the rest of that bunch out after his wife."

"The one who was going to pay out a bunch of money for her?"

"That's him," said Pool. "We got her too, but Slocum run me off. He must still be out here somewhere with her."

"And the old man wonders what's happened. Right?"

"Right. He's on their trail."

"Reckon what's holding Slocum up. He take a fancy to that woman for himself maybe?"

"No, I don't think so," Pool said. "There was some guys from the Big O chasing us. Maybe he had trouble with them. Anything could have held him up. That big storm a few days back. I guess old Hodges just ain't got no patience."

They unsaddled their horses and turned them loose at the creek, but Smythe kept the saddlebags thrown over his shoulder. They were filled with the bank cash, and he didn't want to take a chance on anyone stumbling over them. "Let's go get some of that coffee," he said.

"Just a minute," said Wickson.

"What are you thinking?" said Smythe.

"You heard what we was talking about?"

"Yeah."

"I'm thinking we ought to be able to turn this thing to our advantage somehow."

"We got to get our ass up to Montana," said Smythe.

"Even if that posse does come along," Wickson said, "do you think they'll spot us in amongst all these cowhands?"

Slocum paid for the meal and the bottle and then he got a room for the night for Julia. He checked it out personally, looking out the window to see if there was any way she could escape. Then he left her to turn in for the night. He went out of the room and put a chair in front of her door and sat down on it. He would stay there all night. He didn't worry about Morales and Bradley. Let them take care of themselves. He was still pondering his dilemma. He still had not figured a way out. He took out a cigar and a match and lit up. He had what was left of the bottle of whiskey with him, and he took a sip out of the bottle.

Downstairs, Maxie and Slick still sat at the same table. Morales was still at his table. He was smoking and pouting. Slocum had taken the bottle with him. He wished that Slocum had not found him so drunk after Julia had run away from them.

Slick slipped a pistol out of his belt and held it on his lap. He whispered to Maxie, "Now's our chance."

"You mean, take them now?" said Maxie.

"Slip out your shooter and hold it under the table. We know that one cowboy's up there with Sugar Tits. I'll slip upstairs and check on the other one. You wait for my shot, and then you blast the Mexican."

"I ain't sure—"

"Listen to me. When he hears my shot, he'll turn his attention to the upstairs. It'll be easy for you to get him. Think about all that ransom money that Olaf thinks he's going to get and not share with us."

"All right," said Maxie.

Slick stood up casually. He tucked his six-gun back into his trousers. He stretched and yawned out loud. "Well, be seeing you," he said. He walked toward the stairway, and as he passed by the barkeep, he said, "Good night, Mac."

"See you, Slick," Mac responded.

Morales glanced at Slick as he passed by his table. He continued smoking. Slick walked to the stairs and started up. In a minute, he was up on the landing. He spotted Slocum almost instantly. It surprised him to see the man sitting out in the hallway. He didn't have time to think. He only reacted. He knew what he wanted to do, so he pulled his revolver, raised it and cocked it. Slocum saw him, and threw himself to the floor, drawing his Colt at the same time. Slick's shot was loud in the narrow hallway, but the bullet went wild. Slocum fired once. His bullet caught Slick in the neck, and blood spurted out like water from a spigot. Slick staggered. He stood wavering. Then he fell back and slid halfway back down the stairs. Morales jumped up and headed for the stairway, pulling his gun, but he stumbled and fell on his face, just as Maxie fired a shot that went harmlessly over him. Morales rolled over and fired back at Maxie. His shot tore into Maxie's arm, causing him to drop his gun. Maxie screamed in pain and fright.

Upstairs, Julia called out from her room, "What's going on out there?"

"Just stay where you are," said Slocum.

Bradley peeked out of another room. He was naked, but he held a gun in his hand.

"What's happening?" he said.

"Stay right there and watch this hallway," Slocum said. He ran down to the landing. He saw Slick sprawled out on the stairs. He looked down into the saloon and saw Morales up and all right. "Esteban," he called.

"It's all right, Slocum," said Morales, and he gestured toward Maxie. "I got this son of a bitch. He's only wounded though. You want me to kill him?"

"No. Just let him bleed. And keep an eye on him."

"Okay. I'll do it."

Slocum went back to his post by the door to Julia's room. He looked down the hall to where the naked Bradley still stood in the doorway. "It's all over," Slocum said. "Go on back to your fun." Then he rapped on the door to Julia's room.

"What?" she said.

"It's all right now," he said. "You can go back to sleep." He picked up the whiskey bottle he had dropped when he dodged Slick's bullet. It had not spilled its entire contents. He took a drink. Then he found his cigar on the floor and picked it up. He sat back down in the chair and puffed.

Downstairs, Morales walked over to the wounded Maxie. "You tried to shoot me," he said. "Why did you want to shoot me? Have I ever hurt you?"

"No. No, you ain't."

"Then why?"

"Mister," said Maxie, "I'm hurt. I need tending."

"I ain't going to tend your hurts," said Morales. "Why should I? After you tried to kill me? I would kill you now, but my boss, he said just watch you bleed. So I'm going to sit right down and watch. Maybe you'll bleed to death. It should be interesting. I never watched a man bleed to death before."

He looked where Maxie's six-gun had fallen to the floor, and he kicked it farther away. Then he looked at Maxie's splinted leg. He smiled. He took hold of the chair that Maxie was resting his broken leg on, and he jerked it out. Maxie's foot fell hard to the floor with a heavy thud, and Maxie shrieked in pain. Morales sat down in the chair to watch the man suffer.

14

Wickson, Pool and Smythe sat down with their coffee in the midst of Hodges's cowhands. They knew that a posse was on their trail, but Wickson said that maybe they had been wiped out by that other bunch of riders. He had no idea who they were. Even if the posse had not been wiped out, they might have been shot up badly enough that they had to return to Lost Cause to get patched up. If not, if worse came to worst and they were still on the trail, if they should come across this bunch, the chances were slight that they would spot their prey in the middle of this crowd of cowhands. He had told his two partners that much, but he was thinking even further. He would reserve those thoughts until he'd had a chance to check up on them. He spotted Hodges standing off to one side by himself. That was his chance. He stood up and, carrying his coffee with him, walked over to join the old rancher.

"Say," he said, "I'd like to have a word with you."

Hodges looked suspiciously at the man. He had no idea who this trail bum could be. "Well, go ahead," he said.

"You got quite a big bunch of riders with you."

"So?"

"I was just wondering what you was up to. 'Course, it's none of my business, but—"

"No. It ain't."

119

"Well, I was thinking that maybe we could help each other out."

"I don't know what you three could do for me," said Hodges.

"Can't you tell me what you're riding for?"

"I could."

"But you won't?"

"I can't see any reason why I should."

"One of my pards over there says you're from the Hodges spread. Says you're old man Hodges himself."

"You can tell that from the brands on my horses," Hodges said.

"He says that you're hunting a woman that was stole off your place."

Hodges shot a hard look at Wickson. "You might know a little bit more than is good for you, mister."

"Hey, don't get riled now. I said that we might could help each other out."

"Keep talking."

"Well, one of my pards over there knows the men that took her off of the Big O. Would you know them if you seen them?"

"I'd know them all right."

"You know all of them by sight? They might have separated for some reason, and if you was to come across one or more of them, you might not recognize them. He would. He knows them all."

"All right. And what's in it for you?"

"Oh, nothing special. I figure if we help you out, you might be feeling generous. I ain't looking for no promises there. What I really want is to just hang out with you for a few days. There might be someone on our trail. They don't really know what we look like. They're just chasing three men. If they come on to you and ask if you've seen three men, you could just say that there's no one here but only your hands. That ain't asking much, is it?"

"That man you were talking about. The one who knows the whole bunch. Bring him over here."

"Do we got a deal?" asked Wickson.

"Just bring that man over here."

Wickson walked about halfway back to where Smythe and Pool waited, and he called them to come with him. They got up and started walking to meet him. In the meantime, Hodges called four hands to gather round him. Wickson was a little startled to find five men waiting for them.

"Which one?" said Hodges.

"Pool here," said Wickson, jerking a thumb. "Davey Pool."

"You know who's got my wife, Pool?" Hodges asked.

Pool looked nervously from Hodges to Wickson. Wickson nodded his head vigorously. "Go on," he said. "Tell him."

"Yeah, I know them."

"Well?" said Hodges. "Who the hell are they?"

"The leader's name is Slocum."

"I know that," said Hodges. "I hired the man. You say they rescued my wife?"

"They got her all right."

"How is it that you know that?"

"I was riding with them at first," Pool said, "but Slocum run me off."

"How come?"

Pool thought for a moment. He could not tell the truth about that episode. He looked at Wickson again, but he got no help. "Well," he said, "when we started out, I didn't know what we was up to. Slocum just said he had a job that would pay pretty good, so I went along. Then when I found out the job was stealing a woman, I had an argument with him. I never knew it was your wife. Anyhow, he told me to get out."

Hodges looked at Pool. He believed that Pool knew the men, but he did not believe anything else. He looked at Wickson, and then he looked at Smythe standing by quietly with the heavy saddlebags slung over his shoulder. There was definitely something wrong here. "Boys," he said to the four cowhands standing around him, "take their guns."

"Hold on there," said Wickson, but he was outnumbered,

and in another moment, he and his partners were also un-armed. "What'd you do that for?"

"Find out what they know," said Wickson, and the four cowhands began beating up the three bank robbers. Soon they were joined by other cowhands who formed a circle around the hapless trio. Hodges's cowhands would punch one of the robbers, knocking him across the circle into the hands of another, who would take his turn at punching. Smythe lost the saddlebags right away, and Hodges picked them up. He stepped away from the fun to open them up, and he found them stuffed with money. He walked back over to the melee.

"Hold it, boys," he called out.

The cowhands stopped punching, and Pool and Smythe fell to the ground. Wickson was still standing, but on wobbly legs. All three men had bloody faces. Hodges stepped into the circle and threw the saddlebags to the ground in front of Wickson. Some money spilled out. Pool lifted his head slightly and looked at the money.

"I knowed we should have kept going to Montana," he said.

"All right," said Hodges. "I want the whole story now."

Slocum woke up early the next morning. He rapped on the door to Julia's room and told her to get dressed. He walked down to the room where Bradley had spent the night with Sugar Tits, and he did the same. Then he walked down the stairs. He found Morales awake and staring at Maxie, who was either asleep or passed out. He noticed that Maxie's arm had been wrapped up in some rags. He could tell that Maxie had lost considerable blood. Morales heard Slocum coming and turned to look. "Good morning, Slocum," he said.

"How's it going?" Slocum said.

Morales stood up and held his arms out to his side. "Look," he said. "I am as sober as a judge. Well, some judges."

"Some of the judges I've known," said Slocum. "That ain't saying much." He nodded toward Maxie. "What about him?"

Morales shrugged. "I didn't kill him," he said. "You told me not to. That barkeep came out after a while with some rags and bandaged the arm. He said there ain't no doctor around here. That one cried and whined for a while, but then he went to sleep. Or passed out. Maybe he died. I don't know."

Slocum looked at the wretch with a shot-up arm and a broken leg. "He's not going to bother anyone for a while," he said. "Let's get ready to ride."

Olaf Johnson was wringing his hands, trying to get them loose from the rope that bound them, but they were tied just too tight. He was making no progress. Jugs sat quietly whimpering next to him. "Hey," said Johnson, "can you get your hands loose?"

"Them cowboys tied them too tight," said Jugs. "I think they cut off my circulation. I can't even feel nothing in my hands."

"Shit," said Johnson.

"Olaf?" said Jugs. "Shouldn't you be saying a prayer for us? We're going to die here. Ain't we? We're fixing to hang to death."

"You ain't dead till you're dead," said Johnson. "Now, shut up and start figuring how we're going to get loose from this."

Jugs's horse was grazing. The grass seemed better a little farther ahead. She took a couple of steps forward causing Jugs to lean back and the noose to tighten just a little around his neck. "Oh," he said. "Whoa there, old horse. Whoa now. Back up." The horse took a couple more casual steps forward. "Olaf, this horse is fixing to hang me. Do something."

"What can I do?" said Johnson.

The horse wandered a bit farther, and Jugs slid behind the saddle. "Oh, damn it. I'm sitting clean back on his ass," he said. "Olaf, make her back up." The horse stood still, having found good grass.

"Keep quiet," said Johnson. "You're just egging him on."

The horse stepped forward again, and this time Jugs slipped off behind. There was no sudden drop. He was swinging and choking. "Oh," he cried. "Aaag. Aack." The words were choked out of him first. He kicked his feet. He twisted wildly. Soon the breath was all choked out as well, and then he just dangled, still spinning a bit, lifeless. Olaf Johnson glanced to his left. Now there were two dead men hanging next to him. Now with no one left to cuss at, he was completely alone. He began to feel for sure that he too would die there. He glanced up in the sky to see buzzards circling, and he felt the cold chill of death wrap around him like a shroud. "Oh, Lord," he shouted to the sky, "damn all their heathen souls to hell." His horse moved under him, and he lowered his voice. "Take it easy there," he said. "Ain't no call for you to get excited. Keep calm. Just keep calm, old horse."

The combined forces of Boone Conley and Sheriff Hardy came across Olaf Johnson sitting in his saddle, his head drooped and sagging and next to him the dead and dangling bodies of his two last companions. Johnson heard the horses and lifted his head. He could scarcely believe his good fortune. He tried to speak, but his voice was almost gone, scratchy and hoarse.

"Don't try to talk," said Hardy. "A couple of you boys get him down from there."

Two posse members rode forward. One took out a knife and reached out to cut the rope while the other held Johnson steady in the saddle. Two more men dismounted and went to help Johnson down after the rope had been cut. When the old man's feet touched the ground, his knees buckled and he fell over on his side. The man with the knife cut the ropes that bound his wrists, and then another came forward with a canteen of water. Johnson gulped greedily. Hardy got down out of his saddle and stepped forward.

"Just take it easy, old-timer," he said. He looked back over his shoulder. "We might just as well rest our horses here for a spell."

"Climb down, boys," said Conley.

Johnson looked around. He saw the badge on Hardy's vest, and he saw that he was surrounded by a large group of riders. Then he saw a brand on one of the horses. It was the brand of the Big O Ranch. He decided that he would have to be very careful what he said to his rescuers.

"Who did this to you?" Hardy asked.

Johnson made some gritty, gurgling sounds, pretending that he could not yet speak.

"That's all right," said Hardy. "You can tell us later. Say, a couple of you boys cut down those other two and bury them. We can't leave them just hanging there like that."

Hodges had made his boys beat the shit out of Pool, Wickson and Smythe so much that Hodges had at last decided that he knew everything Pool knew. He had gotten out of Pool that he had actually been with Slocum and the others when they stole Julia away. He had learned what he'd already suspected, that the Big O had sent two separate groups of riders out. O'Neill himself was leading one bunch. And he had learned the real reason for Slocum's dismissing of Pool. When Pool made that fatal admission, Hodges himself had pulled out his six-gun and shot Pool to death. Then he walked away from the crowd to think.

Julia ought to be safe if Slocum was protecting her like that. The only thing he had to worry about was where she was. He hoped she was still with Slocum and that neither bunch of Big O riders had caught up with them. He was unsure of which direction to search. He had the money that those three sorry bank robbers had gotten out of the bank at Lost Cause, and he knew that there was a posse in pursuit of them. He also knew that a large bunch of riders had gotten into a fight with the posse, thus allowing the robbers to escape. He wondered if it could have been one of the Big O bunches. If so, the violent encounter had been a fluke, an accident.

Hodges's pride was hurt bad by the loss of his wife. He had not told anyone, but he, of course, knew that she had not been kidnapped. He knew that she had willingly run away with Loren O'Neill because she could not stand life with Hodges. He did not love her, but she was a beautiful woman, and she was his property. He could not stand for people to know that he had lost her. He wasn't sure, but he suspected that others also knew the truth. He had to get her back. He had to teach her a lesson that she would not soon forget.

Simp Culley walked over to where Hodges brooded. "Boss," he said, "what do you want us to do with them other two men? And with the money?"

Hodges thought about that. The two men had seen him murder their companion. Even if the man was a bank robber, if anyone were to find out about that, he would be made to stand trial for murder. The man had been unarmed. And he did not want to be burdened with two prisoners anyway.

"Throw that saddlebag with the money in it over your own horse," he said. "We'll figure out what to do with it later."

"Okay," said Culley. "And the two men?"

"Shoot them."

Culley walked back to where the two waited. He could see that they were apprehensive, worried about their fate.

"What are you going to do with us?" Wickson asked. "All we done was to just rob a bank. You can't hold that against us. We wasn't with Pool when him and those others stole your boss's woman. We ain't never even laid eyes on her. Why don't you just give us back our money and leave us go? We was headed for Montana."

Culley pulled out his revolver. "You boys all take out your guns," he said. The rest of the cowboys drew their weapons. "If we all shoot them, then no one can talk about the others."

"Wait a minute," said Wickson.

"You can't do that," said Smythe.

"Hey," said Wickson. "What if you keep the money? Just let us ride out. That's all."

A bullet from Culley's revolver shut Wickson's mouth for good. Then all hell broke loose. Bullets riddled the bodies of both men. It took a while for them to fall to the ground, there were so many bullets hitting them, holding them up, but when they finally fell, they were dead for sure. Hodges stepped over and looked at them for a moment. "Mount up, boys," he said. "Let's ride."

15

Slocum was again riding out ahead of Esteban Morales, Bucky Bradley and Julia, scouting the trail, when he topped a rise that was covered with trees and thick brush, offering cover. He saw riders down below heading more or less in his direction. He stopped, keeping himself hidden in the trees, and watched until he recognized them. It was Asa Hodges and some of his hands. Slocum considered riding down to meet them, but something caused him to hesitate. He wondered why Hodges was riding out. It had been some time since Slocum had taken off to bring Julia home. Maybe Hodges had simply lost his patience and come out to investigate. But Slocum wondered if the man had brought the twenty thousand dollars along with him. That did not seem likely. The deal had been for Slocum to bring Julia home. Was the old man planning to double-cross Slocum? From all he had heard about Hodges, that seemed a distinct possibility. He decided that he did not want to meet up with Asa Hodges out on the open range. He would do his best to deliver Julia to the ranch like he had promised, and if they should arrive at the ranch before Hodges returned, well, that would be all right. It would give Slocum a chance to think a little longer about how to handle the situation.

Hodges had enough men with him that, if he should feel so inclined, he could have Slocum, Bradley and Morales gunned down right there, take his wife home to beat her and save himself twenty thousand dollars. That seemed enough of a possibility that Slocum did not want to chance it. He sat and watched a little longer, calculating the direction Hodges was riding and the speed at which he was traveling. He finally figured that if he sat still, Julia and Bradley and Morales would come riding up behind him and catch up with him where he waited, while Hodges and his bunch would ride right past without ever spotting any of them. He stayed put and waited. In a few minutes, Hodges and the others were out of sight. He worried lest his calculations had been wrong. If Hodges were to come across Julia and the other two men while Slocum sat alone in the trees, Slocum would likely lose everything. But just then he heard the sound of approaching horses. He moved slowly out of the trees and around until he saw Morales coming up. Right behind him were Julia and Bradley. Slocum breathed a sigh of relief. He waited for them to ride up even with him.

"Let's go on," he said. "Hodges and some of his hands just rode by heading away from the ranch."

"We're going back to the ranch with him out here?" said Julia.

"It seems like the smartest move," said Slocum. "Come on."

"What about our money?" Bradley asked.

"You think he'd ride out here with it?"

"Well, no, but—"

"Then let's go back to the ranch and wait for him there," said Slocum.

Sheriff Hardy had waited for some time. He decided that it had been long enough and that Johnson should be able to talk. He was curious about who it was that had left him and the other two men hanging like that. It seemed like a particularly cruel way to do someone in. Johnson was sipping a cup of coffee and sitting by a small fire. The rest of Hardy's posse and Conley and all his men were sitting around or pacing impatiently. A few had stretched out to catch a nap while they had a chance. Hardy moved to the fire and sat down beside the wretched old man.

"Can you talk now?" he said.

"I think so," Johnson answered, his voice still harsh and throaty.

"Who did this to you?"

The shifty old bastard lied. He knew that O'Neill and his cowboys had been partners with the bunch that was now riding with the sheriff. "I don't know," he said. "It was a bunch of cowboys. I didn't know them. I guess they was looking for cow thieves and thought we was them. They didn't need no proof. They was a mean bunch. I never run across meaner. They just left us setting on our horses all trussed up like that. Eventual, them other two horses just walked off out from under my two ole pardners." He sniffled a bit then. "Poor ole Jugs and Callaway. It was pretty awful. I can tell you that much. They was good men, both of them. I figured I was going the same way, but the Lord sent you along just in time. Praise the Lord."

"I'm trailing three bank robbers," said Hardy. "Have you seen any sign out here of three men riding alone?"

The old man thought hard. Bank robbers could mean even more money out here. In his mind, he was counting money. The money from the bank robbery and the money from old Asa Hodges. His luck couldn't be all bad. It had to change sometime. Some of that money, if not all of it, just had to come his way. "No," he said, "I can't say I have. Wish I could help you after what all you done for me, but I just ain't run across them. How much money did they get away with?"

"I didn't wait to find out," said Hardy.

"Likely cleaned out your little bank, huh? That's too bad."

"Well," said Hardy, "we have to be going. You can ride along with us if you want to."

"If you don't mind, Sheriff," said Johnson, "I'm still just a bit woozy. I'll just set here awhile and get myself back together. Then I'll ride on home to Bentley."

"Are you sure about that?"

"I'll be all right now. Thank you kindly."

Hardy stood up and looked around for Conley. When he spotted him, he walked over to speak to him. "The old man's going to go on home by himself," he said. "I'm ready to ride. How about you?"

"We just been waiting for you," Conley said.

"All right then. Let's get going."

Johnson sat by the fire sipping coffee while the others all got mounted and rode away. He was trying to think how to turn the situation to his advantage. Riding off from him were two separate groups who had joined together quite by accident. One was hunting the girl that Asa Hodges had promised to pay for. The other was hunting escaped bank robbers. There was money at the end of each trail. Johnson was all alone except for three horses, his own and those of the two hanged men. The group that had just left him was much too big to deal with, and then there was that other bunch out there somewhere, the one that had strung him and Jugs and Callaway up and left them that way. He was still harboring thoughts of revenge. And there was still the bunch that had stolen the girl from the Big O Ranch. There just had to be some way to deal wisely with this situation, some way to turn things to his advantage. He was all alone now, and there was good and bad to that. The odds were now stacked high against him, but if he managed to get his hands on any of that ready cash, he would not have to share it with anyone. He liked that thought all right.

Asa Hodges and his men came up on Bentley. Hodges decided that they could afford to stop for a spell and get a good meal, maybe even have a few drinks. He could question the inhabitants of this sorry place and find out if anyone had ridden through. Then they would get on their way. The whole bunch rode up in front of the saloon, dismounted and tied their horses. "Simp," he said, "have a couple of the boys see that the horses gets watered."

"Right, Boss," said Culley.

Hodges walked on through the front door of the saloon. He was followed by the rest of his hands. Mac looked up from behind the bar, surprised to see so many men coming in the place. He thought, in fact, they had seen quite a few strangers in there lately. "What can I do for you gents?" he asked.

"Whiskey all around," said Hodges. "And you got any grub?"

"Got a big pot of stew on," Mac answered.

"Dish that up all around too," said Hodges.

Mac got busy pouring drinks, and Sugar Tits sidled up to one of the cowhands. Hodges took note. "We ain't got time for that," he said. "Come over here, gal."

Sugar Tits walked over to Hodges and smiled up at him. The scowl never left his rugged, old face. He pulled out a few bills, and Sugar Tits's face lit up.

"You seen any strangers around here lately?" Hodges asked.

"Seen a few," she said.

"Tell me about them."

Sugar Tits told Hodges about the two cowhands who had come in and had a few drinks, then partook of her favors and run away without paying. She told him how old Olaf Johnson and some other men had gone after them. Only two of them had returned, she said. One was killed and the other one was sitting wounded right over there across the room. She pointed out Maxie, who was passed out at the same table he had been at for some time. His broken leg was propped up again on the chair. Then she told him about Slocum, the two riders and Julia. He grabbed her hard by the shoulders.

"You say they spent the night here?" he demanded.

"Hey," she said, "turn a-loose of me. You're hurting me."

He released his grip. "I'm sorry," he said. "Tell me about them."

"They got the woman a room upstairs. One of the boys stayed with me all night in my room. I don't know what the other two done. Mac might know."

Hodges handed her some money, then called Mac over.

Mac had already gotten everyone a drink and was busy dishing out stew.

"That'll wait," said Hodges. "Get over here."

Mac walked over to where Hodges waited. "What is it?" he said.

"The night the men with the woman came in here," Hodges said. "One of the men went with this gal all night. They got the woman a room. What did the other two men do?"

He had visions swirling in his head about Julia and Slocum and whoever the other man was, and they were making him mad. He could not stand the thought of another man with his wife. She belonged to him. If he found out that she had spent the night with either of the men, he would kill her. Then he would kill the other man.

"Well," said Mac, "one of them sat right over there the whole night. That was after he shot ole Maxie in the arm. The other one was setting in a chair in the hall just outside of the woman's room. Like he was guarding her. Slick, ole Maxie's pardner, went upstairs, and that feller out in the hall shot him dead."

"That's all?" said Hodges.

"Hell," said Mac, "ain't it enough?"

"The woman spent the entire night in her room unmolested?"

"I thought it was kind of funny," Mac said. "A woman traveling with three men like that. But that's how it went."

Hodges tossed a bill on the counter. "All right," he said. "Get on back to dishing out that stew. We're in a bit of a hurry."

Apparently Slocum was honorable. That much was good. But Hodges still had unanswered questions. He looked over at the sleeping man with the broken leg and bloody arm. He reached for the bottle on the bar and poured his glass full. Then he took the glass and walked to the table where Maxie slumped. He pulled up a chair and reached over to punch Maxie on the shoulder. Maxie rolled his head and mumbled. Hodges shook him by the shoulder and sent shocks of pain down the wounded arm. Maxie's head popped up.

"Ow," he said. "Hey. Damn it."

"Never mind all that," said Hodges. "I've got some questions for you."

"What kind of questions? What the hell is this all about?"

"How come you to get all shot up like this?" said Hodges. "And how'd you get that broke leg?"

"Who are you, mister?"

Hodges pulled out his revolver. He held it out for a minute, and then he let it drop on the broken leg. Maxie howled in pain. "Just answer my questions," Hodges said. "How'd you get all banged up like this?"

Maxie moaned and groaned and sniffled a bit before he started to talk. "It all started when two cowboys come in here," he said. "They diddled Sugar Tits all night long, and then they never paid her. They run off. Olaf told us to go with him and catch them, so we did. There was six of us: Olaf, his brother Sven, me, Slick and Jugs and Callaway. We caught them, and Olaf was going to hang them, but they begged us not to and said they was after a whole bunch of money. So we let them live and went with them."

"Where was they going to get this money?" Hodges asked.

"From some old rancher whose wife had been stoled," Maxie said. "They had been with the gang that had stoled her back, they said, and whenever they returned her to her husband, he was going to pay big-time for her. Olaf decided that we would be the ones to take her home, but when we got out to the shack where she was supposed to be, she was already gone. We followed two men out of there, but they blowed us up with dynamite. Killed Sven and knocked Slick silly and broke my leg. So Olaf, he sent me and Slick back here, and they went on. That's the last I know till them three come by here with the woman. I guess it was her. She didn't act like she was with none of them. Not really with them, if you get my meaning. Well, one of the boys went upstairs with Sugar Tits, and one of them went up to guard the woman. He had got her a room, you know."

Maxie stopped talking. He was thinking, wondering if he'd told too much. Hodges lifted the revolver up over his leg again.

"Don't do that," said Maxie. "I was just thinking. Well, about then ole Slick, he said to me, that was our chance. You know, to get the gal and take her back to her old man for the reward. He was going upstairs to take care of the one man, and I was supposed to get the other one, a Mexican. He went on up, and I heard a shot, and I tuck a shot at the Mex, but I missed him, and he shot me in the arm. Then Slick come a-tumbling down the stairs shot dead. That's the whole story, mister. I swear it. 'Cept that they all packed up in the morning and tuck out of here. That's all."

Hodges leaned back in his chair and heaved a sigh. He stood up, holstered his gun and looked around the room. "You boys ready to ride?" he called out.

"When you say," Culley answered.

"Get mounted up then," Hodges said. He turned back toward Maxie. "Those men were working for me," he said. "They were on their way to my place with my wife, and you interfered with them. I ought to kill you."

He kicked a leg of Maxie's chair, knocking it out from under him. Maxie landed hard on the floor, his one foot still propped up on the other chair. He howled as he fell, and Hodges turned and walked out of the saloon.

Back behind the bar, Mac shook his head slowly. "We ain't had this much excitement in Bentley in a hell of a long time," he said.

"Ow, Mac," whimpered Maxie, "come over here and help me back up into the chair. That old son of a bitch like to've killed me. Ow, damn, I'm hurting bad."

It was just a few minutes later when Olaf Johnson came walking in. Mac had already gotten Maxie back up in his chair and brought him another bottle of whiskey. Johnson saw Maxie and the bottle. He asked Mac for another glass and went over to sit with Maxie.

"Where's everyone else at?" Mac asked.

"All dead and gone," said Johnson. "Gone to their final reward."

He poured his glass full of whiskey.

"Jugs and Callaway?" said Maxie.

"I damn near went with them," said Johnson, and he told the tale of what O'Neill had done to them, and how long he had spent in the saddle with the noose around his neck. He told also about what O'Neill had done earlier, leaving them barefoot with no horses and no guns.

"That's awful," said Maxie.

"I'll get that O'Neill yet," Johnson said. He drained the whiskey out of his glass and poured a refill.

"Well," said Maxie, "things ain't exactly been quiet around here while you was out."

"Oh, yeah?" said Johnson. "Tell me about it."

Maxie told Johnson about Slocum's visit: that he'd had the woman with him, and how Slick got killed and he got a bullet in his arm.

"And that on top of my broke leg and all," he said.

"God damn," said Johnson. "You mean she was here? Right here?"

"She was right here, all right," said Maxie. "That's what got me shot and Slick kilt."

"Damn it all to hell," said Johnson. "And me a-setting out there on the back of that damn horse with my neck in a noose praying to the Lord to save my sorry ass."

"And then just a while ago," Maxie said, "another bunch come in. I didn't have no idea who they was, but the old man what was leading them got to asking questions. He asked Sugar Tits and Mac and then he come over here and tortured me till I talked to him."

"What kind of questions?"

"He wanted to know if any strangers had been in here, and it turned out that he was the man who is looking to have his wife brought back to him. It was him, for sure."

"Old man Hodges," said Johnson.

"That's right. And just before he left, he said that we had been interfering with his hired hands what was bringing her home, and he kicked my chair out from under me."

16

"Hey, Slocum," said Morales. "Look over there. What do you think?"

Slocum looked where Morales was pointing and saw a family of coyotes nuzzling something on the ground. "I don't know," he said. "Let's check it out."

They rode closer, and then they could see some human legs sticking out from the bunch of snarling beasts. Slocum pulled out his rifle and took a shot, killing one of the coyotes and scaring the rest off. They rode on in. Soon they could see that there were two bodies. When they got even closer, Slocum looked over at Julia. "You might want to hang back," he said. "It ain't going to be pretty."

"All right," she said.

"Bucky," said Slocum. "You stay here with her."

Slocum and Morales rode on up to the two bodies. They had not been mangled too badly yet by the coyotes. Slocum did not recognize either man. Morales was looking around some more, and pretty soon he came across another body. "Over here, Slocum," he said. Slocum rode over to see what Morales had found. "It's Davey," Morales said.

"By God," said Slocum, recognizing the remains of Davey Pool.

"I wonder who them other two was," said Morales, "that he fell in with."

"Whoever they were," said Slocum, "they were bad company. What can you tell about this place?"

"A group of riders stopped here. They built a small fire over there. Then they rode out that way."

"After killing these three," said Slocum.

"It looks that way all right."

"From the direction they went," said Slocum, "I'd say that it was Hodges and his crew."

"I'd almost bet money on it," Morales agreed.

"Let's get out of here," Slocum said. They rode back to where Bradley and Julia waited, and then they kept riding toward Hodges's ranch. Slocum was thinking now that he had all the more reason for not leaving Julia with Hodges. From the way it looked back there, the three men had been murdered. He did not see a gun beside any one of them. Davey Pool was shot only once from the front, but the other two were riddled with bullets. Hodges had a bunch of men with him, and it sure did look like they had not given these three a chance in hell. Slocum did not have a clear set of plans, but he intended getting Julia back to the ranch before Hodges and his men returned. He intended to collect his money, and he did not intend to leave her there when he left.

Hardy and Conley had an argument over which way to ride, so in the end they decided to split up. After all, they weren't after the same thing anyhow. They had been sort of following the trail of the bank robbers, but it had mostly petered out. Hardy still thought that he knew which way they had gone, and he meant to stay on that trail. Conley did not think that O'Neill and his bunch of Big O riders were going that same way. He had not yet seen any sign of them. So the two groups split and went in different directions. Hardy, of course, had no way of knowing, but he was headed in a direction that would lead him directly into the path of Slocum.

Back at Bentley, old Olaf Johnson had himself a big meal. He took two bottles of whiskey and several boxes of ammunition. Then he got a fresh horse and left town again. He was on the trail of money. He could smell it. That's all he had to do, just keep following his nose. He had not been out too long when he came across the bodies of Pool, Smythe and Wickson. He stopped and studied them for a bit, drank a few gulps of whiskey, then, puzzled, got back on his horse and headed on. He thought, Things are getting downright dangerous out on this prairie.

Sheriff Hardy saw Slocum and the others up ahead. He cautioned his posse to keep their guns in their holsters. He did not want to risk another shoot-out with the wrong people. They had been lucky the last time. No one had been hit. "Be ready for anything though," he said. They kept riding.

From the other direction, Slocum had spotted the posse. He squinted at them for a few seconds. "Morales," he said. "Do you recognize anyone?"

"No," said Morales. "I don't think so. They're riding easy, and they ain't going for their guns."

"Yeah," said Slocum. "Don't do anything rash, but be ready, just in case."

"They outnumber us pretty bad," said Bradley.

"I can see a badge on that man's vest," Julia said. She was asking herself if she should throw herself on the mercy of the law. This was a new twist to the whole affair. What would the law do? She decided that the law would likely deliver her back to Asa Hodges, and she did not want that, so she decided to keep quiet.

"You're right," said Slocum. "Just take it easy, boys."

They stopped and waited for the posse to approach. As he rode in, Sheriff Hardy was looking at them suspiciously, but the first thing he noticed was Slocum's big Appaloosa. He knew that none of the bank robbers had ridden that. And then he saw Julia. He remembered that Conley and his bunch had been looking for a kidnapped woman. "Howdy," he said.

"You look like you're out on business," said Slocum.

"You might say that," said Hardy. "We're chasing three men that robbed our bank at Lost Cause. What might you be up to?"

"We're just escorting this lady to her home," Slocum said. "This is Mrs. Hodges. She and her husband own the Hodges Ranch."

"I know the place," said Hardy. He also knew that riders from the Big O were looking for this same woman, but he thought he'd just keep quiet about that. It really was none of his business. "I don't suppose you've seen anything of three riders out this way?"

"We saw three dead men back down the trail there," Slocum said. "It looked like they'd been murdered and left for the coyotes and buzzards."

"Did you bury them?" Hardy asked.

"Didn't have the time."

"I don't reckon you found any money?"

"If they're your bank robbers," Slocum said, "then whoever killed them got your money. We never saw any sign of it."

"I hope you won't mind if we check your saddlebags," Hardy said.

"I guess it wouldn't do any harm," Slocum said.

Hardy had a couple of men dismount and walk over to check the bags. "Nothing, Sheriff," said one of the men, walking back to his horse.

"I didn't expect so," Hardy said. "Had to check though. You understand."

"Sure," said Slocum. "We'll be riding on."

"Not just yet. I'd like for you to ride along with us to where you found them bodies."

"You'll come across them with no trouble," Slocum said. "Just—"

"I'd like for you to ride along," said Hardy.

Slocum shrugged. "We'll backtrack a spell," he said to his three companions.

When they came across the bodies, the coyotes were back. The sheriff and some of his posse men shot them. Then they rode on up. The bodies were in worse shape than they had been before, but they were still recognizable. "That's them all right," Hardy said. "Well, boys, all we're looking for now is our money. Let's get these three buried."

"Any reason to keep us hanging around?" Slocum asked.

"When you come across these," said Hardy, "did you see anything else?"

"Sheriff," said Slocum, "we've come across the whole damn country out here. There's a bunch of riders out there somewhere from the Big O Ranch that don't want us to get this lady home. Then there's a scruffy bunch from Bentley riding around thinking they're going to get some money from someone."

"I run onto the Big O boys," said Hardy. "We was down south of here."

Morales looked at Slocum. "I don't think so," he said.

"South of here?" said Slocum. "That's the ones we left behind in the valley. So there's two bunches of them. The latest now is that Hodges has led some of his boys out here looking for us." He hesitated, wondering how much he should tell. "I think they were right here not long ago."

"Hodges was?"

"That's right."

"Before or after these men was killed?"

Slocum gave Morales a look. "I studied the ground," Morales said. "I would say that they killed these three."

"God damn," said the sheriff. "Then Hodges has got our money."

"That's likely," said Slocum. "Now can we get on our way?"

Hardy wracked his brain, but he could not think of any further reason to hold on to Slocum and the others, so he let them go. Then he continued on his way after Hodges.

A little farther west, Conley's Big O riders and O'Neill's Big O riders came across one another. They decided to stop and rest and get each other's stories. O'Neill asked Conley, "Where the hell have you been? We were supposed to catch that bunch between us."

"We come through that narrow pass back yonder," said Conley, "and they blowed it up. Trapped us there. We had to ride back till we come to a place where we could turn south and then head on back this direction. Then we run across a sheriff and his posse chasing some bank robbers and got in a fight with them. They thought that we was the robbers. Lucky no one was killed. When we figured it all out, we rode along with them for a spell. We just split up a while ago, and then we finally come on you."

"We thought that we had them," said O'Neill, "till that big storm hit, and then we lost them. We haven't seen anyone since then but some old farts from a little dump called Bentley. We fixed them up though. They won't be bothering anyone again."

"So what do we do now?"

"I'd say we quit farting around and head directly for old Hodges's place."

"There's likely to be a big fight if we go there."

"Could be," said O'Neill. "But the kidnappers've had time to get her back there by now, and we're just floundering around out here."

"Loren," said Conley, "having that man's wife over at your place, that's one thing, but shooting it out with him at his own home is something else. The law will be clearly on his side if anyone gets killed."

"Well, that's what we're going to do," said O'Neill. "The old bastard don't deserve her. He treats her mean. And she don't want him neither."

Conley paced away, shaking his head. "I don't know," he said.

"You don't have to know, Boone," said O'Neill. "Tell you what. I bet my old man is worrying and wondering about us. I got enough boys with me to do the job. You take your bunch and go on back to the ranch. Tell Papa that we're okay, and we'll be along home directly. I'm sure there's plenty of work to be done around the place anyhow, and I've kept too many hands out for too long."

"You sure, Loren?"

"Just do what I say," said O'Neill. "Take your boys and go back to the ranch." • • •

Olaf Johnson had not seen anyone along the trail other than the three dead men. He was puzzling about where they could all be. Up ahead he saw the hill with the trees and brush covering it, and he stopped to study it. He took out a bottle and sucked on it. Then he corked it and put it back in his bag. He rode on to the top of the hill. From here, he thought, he should be able to see anything that was going on for several miles around in all directions. He went to the far side of the hill and studied the terrain all around. He saw a group of riders heading west, a pretty large group. He thought about O'Neill and those that had done him so wrong. He reached into his saddlebags and pulled out a spyglass. Sliding it out full length, he put it to his eye and studied the riders. He did not recognize them. Of course, he had never run across Conley and his bunch. He lowered the glass. He guessed that it did not matter who they were. They were headed west anyway. He could not see anyone else. Keeping the spyglass in his hand, he rode back to the east side of the hill and took a look around. There was another gang of riders, a smaller bunch. He was pretty sure that it was not O'Neill's bunch. That was a larger crowd. He looked through the spyglass. Again he did not know who he was looking at. He lowered the glass, and then he got a big surprise. There was another bunch coming up behind the smaller one. He raised the glass again, and again they were strangers to him. He put down the glass and tried to think.

There was no woman with either bunch, so it could not be the bunch that had her. There was that damned posse out after bank robbers. Could he be watching the pursuit? He looked through the glass again. It was not the posse. He thought too that the first bunch was too big to be the bank robbers. He wondered if he had come across the bank robbers back down the trail—the three dead men he had found. If so, someone else had the money. He had not seen any sign of it. The two groups down below did not make any sense at all to Johnson, but he figured they had to be of some interest. There was the old man with all the money, promised for the return of his wife, and there was the money from the bank robbery. These two bunches of riders had to have something to do with one or the other. There just was never so much activity in these parts before. He decided to take a chance. He mounted up and rode slowly and easily down the side of the hill, allowing the first group of riders to come up on him as if by surprise.

Hodges had a rifle in his hands. The whole bunch of riders stopped. "Who are you, mister?" Hodges demanded.

Johnson saw the big "H" on the flank of the horse. His shifty eyes looked for other brands, and every one he saw was the same. He tried to recall just what Maxie had told him about the visits he'd had in Bentley. One had been from old man Hodges, and Maxie had told the old son of a bitch too much, had probably given Johnson's name to Hodges. Johnson thought that he had just been confronted by Hodges himself. He figured he had to be careful what he said. Maxie said that Hodges had tortured him to get information.

"Just a lone wanderer, mister," he said.

"What's your name?"

"Why, uh, Carl Evans," Johnson lied.

"Where'd you come from?"

"Up north. Wyoming."

"Where you headed?"

"Don't rightly know, mister. I'm kind of looking for work."

"Just what kind of work do you do?"

"I've done most anything," Johnson said. "I've worked cows. Done some mining. Been a hide hunter."

"You won't find hunting very good around here," Hodges said. "Have you seen any riders around here?"

"Not lately," said Johnson. "Couple of days ago there was a big bunch from a place called the Big O Ranch. A mean bunch they was. I had a couple of partners, and they tuck us for cow thieves. Hanged my two pards."

"How'd you get away?"

"Just lucky is all. They said they was looking for a woman that had been stoled off their ranch."

"They're lying sons of bitches," said Hodges. "The

woman is my wife, and they are the thieves. I'm looking for her now."

"Oh my," said Johnson. "Well, she must've been double stole then."

"I sent a man named Slocum to rescue her and bring her home," Johnson said. "I suspect that he got her all right, but he hasn't showed up at my ranch yet."

"Say, I was in a little town called Bentley not long ago," Johnson said. "I heard about him. They said that a man called Slocum had come through there with two other men and a woman. I betcha that was her."

Old Hodges was about to get excited, but just then Hardy and his posse appeared riding up behind them.

"Who the hell is that?" Hodges said.

Johnson gestured toward the top of the hill. "There's cover up yonder," he said.

17

Johnson and Hodges and the posse all rode like hell to the top of the hill. All of the men quickly dismounted, allowing their horses to wander into the woods loose. They had all grabbed their rifles first, of course. Finding whatever cover they could find, behind trees or rocks or down on their bellies in the tall grass, they held their weapons ready and waited. Johnson did not want to take any chances. When the posse was nearly close enough to recognize, he shouted.

"I think that's that goddamned Big O bunch," he said, and he fired a shot which knocked one of the riders out of his saddle. Down below, the posse hustled for cover. Someone helped the wounded man in too. Immediately they began to return fire.

"Who the hell is that up there?" said Hardy. "The bank robbers is already killed."

"I'm damned if I know," said the man closest to him, "but they're sure as hell trying to kill us."

"It must be that Hodges, and they must have the bank money," Hardy said. "Why else would any damn fool open up on a posse?"

Up on the hill Johnson had figured out that whoever was down there, it was not the Big O riders, and he decided that he had better get the hell out of there quick. Hodges and the others were all busy shooting. He stayed low and sneaked back into the woods. He looked around for his horse, but he couldn't spot it. He decided to just take the first horse he could catch, and he grabbed one as he came up to it. He mounted as fast as he could and rode toward the back side of the hill. He wanted to get away from the fight, but he did not want to get too far away from the area because of all the money that was floating around. He rode hard until the sounds of the shots behind him had faded. Then he looked around for a shady spot and stopped to rest the horse. He checked the saddlebags and found a little hard bread. He tore off a piece and ate it. Then he took the canteen and had a drink of water. He cursed for not having found his own horse, because he had two bottles of whiskey in his bags there.

He noted with curiosity that this horse was wearing an extra pair of saddlebags. He opened up that pair and was astonished to find both sides packed with money. He could scarcely believe his good fortune. "God damn lordy Jesus," he exclaimed. "I'm a rich son of a bitch. A rich son of a bitch." He longed for some whiskey so he could drink to his good fortune. He danced a little jig, but that wore him out quickly. Then he sat down in the grass, clutching the saddle-bags to his chest, and started to think.

He had stolen someone's horse from that Hodges crew. If he was real lucky, maybe that son of a bitch, whoever he was, would get killed in the fight. Then he wondered how long the fight would continue. When it was over, would someone come looking for him? He would be in big trouble with a stolen horse and the stolen bank money. He decided that he could head for Mexico. He would have to be careful to avoid all the different assholes that were running around this country like headless chickens, but if he could manage it, he could live like a king down there for the rest of his life.

He did need some whiskey though. He would have to backtrack and go through Bentley. That was all there was to it. It was the nearest whiskey. He had no other choice. He would ride hard and fast to Bentley, ditch the stolen horse, get another, get a good supply of whiskey and head south as fast as he could go, watching carefully along the way for any signs of riders. He mounted up again and turned the stolen horse toward Bentley.

O'Neill and his riders heard the sounds of gunshots up ahead. "Let's go see who that is," said O'Neill, and they whipped up their horses. Up on the hill, Simp Culley was the first to see the large group of riders coming. He nudged Hodges on the shoulder and pointed.

"God damn," said Hodges. "Who the hell is that?"

"I'd bet my ass it's O'Neill," said Culley.

"Then who the hell are we shooting at?"

"Damned if I know."

"Well, hell, we can't fight all of them. Let's grab our horses and get the hell out of here by the back way."

"Boys," shouted Culley, "grab the first horse you can catch. We're riding out of here."

Hodges, Culley and the rest of the Hodges crew moved back into the woods and started scrambling for horses. Culley and another rider got hold of the same horse. "Go find yourself another one," said Culley. "I got this one first."

"But this one is my horse."

"I don't give a shit. I'm riding him."

Down below the hill, Hardy was confused more than ever. The gunfire had stopped. "What the hell is going on now?" he asked.

The next man over shrugged. "There's a bunch of riders coming," he said. "Maybe they scared them off."

Hardy looked at the approaching riders. He hesitated. Just about anyone out here was as likely to start shooting before they'd had any introductions as they were to ask any questions. He waited until the riders were closer and saw that none of them had their guns out. Everything was quiet now except for the sounds of the large bunch of arriving horses. Hardy stood up and waved. O'Neill and his whole gang pulled up.

"Howdy. I'm Sheriff Hardy from Lost Cause."

"Loren O'Neill from the Big O."

"Say," said Hardy, "I rode with a bunch of yours. Fellow named Conley."

"Yeah. They're mine. I sent them on home."

"Had a fight with them too. Lucky no one was hurt before we figured out who was who."

"Yeah," said O'Neill. "Lucky. So was that you doing all that shooting we heard just now?"

"It sure was," said the sheriff. "We were riding along here, and someone drygulched us from up on that hill. Don't know who it was, but I got me an idea. Guess you scared them off."

"Who do you think it was?"

"Well, sir, we was chasing a small gang of bank robbers. Your Conley killed one of them. Then we come across the other three, all killed and left to be et by coyotes. We burried them, but there wasn't no bank money. There was signs that someone else had been there though. A pretty good size bunch it was. Well, for one reason and another, we figured it was old man Hodges done it. Figure he's got that bank money, and I can't figure any other reason for anyone to ambush a posse if he ain't the one it's chasing."

"So you think Hodges is out here with some riders?" O'Neill asked.

"That's what that Slocum said."

"Who's Slocum?"

"Well, I never did get all of that straight in my head, partly because I'm out looking for stolen bank money, but the best I could gather, Slocum has got Hodges's wife and is taking her back to the ranch, but it has took him so long to get back with her that Hodges come out a-looking for himself."

"Slocum's got her?" said O'Neill. "And Hodges doesn't know it?"

Hardy shook his head. "That's sure what I gathered from it all."

"So where is Slocum going with her?"

"Back to her ranch," he said.

Loren O'Neill was tickled pink. If Asa Hodges had the

stolen bank money, then no lawman would be upset when O'Neill killed him, no matter where the killing took place. He could hardly wait to catch up with the bastard.

It was dark by the time Johnson got back to Bentley. He dismounted, taking his rifle and the saddlebags full of money, and let the horse go. Then he went into the saloon. Maxie was still sitting there in the same spot with his broken leg still propped up on the same chair. "Olaf," he said when he saw Johnson come in. "I'm glad you're back. I'm getting lonesome in here."

"Well, you're just going to have to stay lonesome, I reckon, on account of I'm hitting the trail again."

"What the hell for?"

"There's money to be had out there," said Johnson. "Mac, pour me a whiskey and set me two bottles out there for the road."

"You can at least set down and have a drink with me, can't you?" said Maxie.

Johnson took the opened bottle and two glasses and moved over to Maxie's table. He sat down and poured two drinks. He was still clutching the saddlebags.

"What you got there?" Maxie asked.

"Just my extra clothes," said Johnson. "Drink up."

"I never knowed you to pack extra clothes," Maxie said. "In fact, I don't think I've ever knowed you to have anything 'cept what you've got on right now."

"I mean to be out longer than usual," Johnson said. "I had to get me some new duds."

"You didn't have no extra clothes with you when you tuck off last time. Where'd you get them?"

"Just shut up about my clothes and drink your whiskey."

"It's kind of strange," said Maxie. "You hadn't ought to be riding out tonight anyhow. It's dark by now, and the trail'll be some treacherous. Why not wait till morning? We can get drunk tonight."

"No. I can't wait. I got to get rolling here in just a few more minutes. But I got to know something before I leave here."

"What's that?"

"You just been setting here the whole time?"

"I can't get around on this leg. You know that."

"But ain't you even got up to go take a shit or nothing?"

Maxie got a serious pout on his face. "That's getting real personal, Olaf," he said.

"Well, you was asking about my clothes."

"That's different."

"No, it ain't."

"Olaf?" said Maxie. "What you really got in them bags?"

Johnson drained his glass and stood up. "I'm gone," he said. He walked to the bar and picked up the two full bottles, and, still holding tight to the saddlebags, headed for the door. He was about halfway across the room when Maxie slipped his big Remington six-shooter out from under his coat, aimed and cocked it and pulled the trigger. A lead slug tore into the middle of Johnson's back. He winced and jerked and staggered a few small steps forward. Then, drawing his own weapon, he turned to face Maxie. Maxie fired again. His second bullet tore into the saddlebags Johnson was holding. Johnson fired, and his bullet struck Maxie right between the eyes. Maxie's head fell back with a dull and listless expression on the face. Johnson staggered a few steps forward, then fell on his face. He clutched the saddlebags tightly for a couple of seconds. Then his eyes rolled back in his head, and his arms went limp. He was dead.

Mac stood still behind the bar watching with wide open eyes. When he was sure that neither man would move again, he walked around the bar and over to where Johnson lay. Johnson was still, likely dead, but Mac felt like he had to be damned sure. He reached out with a foot and kicked Johnson's gun away. Then he nudged the body. There was no reaction. With his foot, he rolled it over. It was dead. He looked over at Maxie with the hole between his eyes. He was dead. There was no doubt of that. Mac bent over and pulled the saddlebags loose from Johnson's dead carcass. He opened one flap and looked inside. He gasped. He had never seen so much money in his life. He hurried back behind the bar and tucked it out of sight underneath. He had to try to think of what to do.

Just then Sugar Tits came halfway down the stairs. "Mac?" she said. Mac jumped.

"Oh, Sugar Tits," he said.

"I heard shooting," she said.

"That was Olaf and Maxie," said Mac. "They just shot each other dead. Right here in front of me."

"Mercy heavens. What for?"

"Why, uh, I don't know. They just got to arguing and insulting each other, and before I knew what was happening, they was shooting."

She came the rest of the way down the stairs and stared at the two bodies. Then she walked slowly to the bar. Still staring toward Johnson's corpse, she asked Mac, "Would you pour me a drink?

"Sure," he said. "I think I need one too."

He poured two drinks on the bar. Sugar Tits drank one down. Mac polished off the other.

"What're you going to do?" she asked him.

"Well, I ain't for sure. I guess I'll just have to get them outta here and get them buried," he said. "We ain't got no law unless a U.S. marshal happens through. You know that. Besides, if either one of them is guilty of murder, he's already killed. I guess I could just drag them out back and plant them before they get to stinking up the place too bad."

"They both of them stunk bad enough when they was alive," said Sugar Tits. "Lately especially Maxie."

O'Neill and his boys had turned around right quick and headed for Hodges's ranch, and Sheriff Hardy and his posse had taken off on the trail of Hodges and his bunch of hands. He couldn't figure out any other place the stolen bank money might be, except with Hodges. He told himself as they were riding in pursuit that Hodges probably had not intended to steal the money. He just did not want to leave it lying around, and he intended to return it when he got back from his present business. Hardy was not looking for another fight. But then, if it had been Hodges on top of the hill, then Hodges, or someone in his bunch, had fired on the posse earlier. Perhaps it had been another case of mistaken identity. Well, he did not really expect a fight, but still he told the posse to be ready for anything that might happen—just in case.

They caught up with Hodges sooner than Hardy expected. The Hodges crowd had stopped beside a creek and were resting their horses. They had even built a fire and made some coffee. Hodges stood, hands on hips, and watched as the posse approached. Hardy, the posse behind him, stopped just in front of Hodges. "Sheriff," said Hodges, "you and your men climb on down. We got some coffee."

Hardy swung down wearily out of the saddle. "Thanks," he said. "You Hodges?"

"I am, and I expect you're looking for that bank money."

"That's right," Hardy said. "We took off after the robbers, but they're all dead now. The money was gone though."

"I took it," said Hodges.

"Figured you did. If you'll just turn it over to me, we'll consider the matter closed."

Hodges walked toward the fire, and Hardy followed him. A man there at the fire poured a cup full of hot coffee and handed it to the sheriff. Hardy took a tentative sip. The rest of the posse were headed for the coffeepot. Hodges turned away from the fire. "I can't do that," he said.

"How come?"

"When we took it, I had Simp Culley toss the saddlebags on his horse. We run across an old-timer back down the trail. He said his name was Carl Evans. I believed him at the time. Didn't have no reason not to. Then we got in a fight with someone. Don't know who it was, but we saw a large bunch coming to join up with them and decided to hightail it out of there. We was in such a hurry that we didn't get on our own horses. Evans was gone, and so was Simp's horse. I reckon Evans has got the money."

"God damn," said Hardy. "And you got no idea which way he went?"

"Afraid not."

"God damn. Well, I can tell you who it was you was fighting with. It was us."

"You?"

"Hell yes."

"Sorry, Sheriff. I didn't know. That Evans said it was O'Neill and his men. Was anyone hurt?"

"You nicked one of my boys, but he's all right. What did this goddamned Evans look like?"

"Well, he's an old man. Gray hair and beard. He has the look and smell of an old hide hunter, and he's wearing a coat made out of wolf hides, looks like. If you run across him, you'll know him, all right."

"By God," said Hardy, "that sounds like that Olaf Johnson that we saved from hanging."

"Well, you should've let him hang," Hodges said. "Who strung him up?"

"He just said it was a bunch of cowboys. He said he didn't know them."

"Olaf Johnson, huh?" said Hodges. "I heard that name in Bentley. We both missed a chance. I should've killed him right off."

"It sure would've saved a lot of trouble. Now I've got to go hunting him down to find that bank money."

"He had a partner in Bentley. You might try there. Say, if we were shooting at you a while ago, who was that bunch that come up and scared us off?"

"That was Loren O'Neill off the Big O spread west of here." A dark and worried look spread across Hodges's face. Hardy continued, "I expect you'll be wanting to get on back home, Mr. Hodges. From what I understand, that man Slocum has got your lady, and he's headed there right now, but the rest of the news is that O'Neill knows it, and he's on his way there too."

"Did he say that?"

"That's what he said."

"The son of a bitch," said Hodges. "I never thought he'd be bold enough to ride right onto my place like that. Well, by God, we'll be ready for him. He'll have his hands full all right."

18

There wasn't much business in Bentley, hadn't been for several years, and now with Johnson and his gang all gone, Mac just couldn't see any reason for staying around. He had stayed as long as he had simply because he had a little business and no means to get out. Now he had the means. It was stashed under the bar inside the saloon. He was out back digging a deep hole and thinking. He finally had the hole about deep enough, and he scrambled out of it. The two stinking bodies were lying to one side. He had dragged them out the back door. Now he stepped over to them and toppled them one after the other unceremoniously into the hole. He wiped a shirtsleeve across his brow and then took up the shovel again. He began to fill the hole from the pile of dirt he had just created.

Inside the saloon, Sugar Tits was sitting at the bar listlessly sipping a glass of whiskey. She knew what Mac was up to out back. She was thinking about the loss of nearly all of Mac's and her own customers and wondering what would become of the two of them. She knew that she had to get out, but she sure as hell did not have the money to do so. Oh, she had a few dollars tucked away. Maybe she could saddle up one of the horses Johnson and them had left behind, pack some clothes, mount up and ride away. But she did not know where she would ride to. She wasn't even sure of the direction to the nearest town. She tried to recall how she had wound up in Bentley, but it had been so long ago that she couldn't remember the details of the trip.

Mac came back in, mopping his face with his apron. "Got that done," he said. He tossed the apron aside and walked over to sit beside Sugar Tits at the bar. He poured himself a drink.

"What you going to do, Mac?" she asked him.

"I'm clearing out," he said.

"Just like that?"

"Just like that. Ain't nothing to keep me here no longer."

"God. I wish I could do that."

"You can have this place if you want it," Mac said. "'Course it ain't worth much no more."

"Thanks," she said. They sat silent for a moment. "I'll just likely starve to death here."

Mac looked at her. She had been beautiful once. She still wasn't too bad. He himself was not the man he had once been. He knew that. He had a sudden thought. It had been a long time since he had acted on impulse. "Sugar Tits," he said, "you want to go along with me?"

She looked over at him with wide eyes. "Where you going?" she asked.

"I don't really know," he said. "You tell me where you'd like to go, and that's where we'll go."

"Anyplace?"

"Anyplace at all."

"Gee, I've always wanted to see San Francisco, but that's a long ways off. It'd cost lots of money."

"The money's no problem," said Mac. "We'll go to San Francisco. And you won't have to work no more when we get there. We'll just live on easy street."

"It sure sounds nice, but you ain't got that much money."

Mac stood up and walked around behind the bar. He bent over and reached under, then drew out the saddlebags. Walking back to the bar just across from Sugar Tits, he opened the bags up. She looked in, and her jaw dropped.

"Where the hell did you get all that?" she asked.

"This is what them two killed each other over," he said. "Now they're both dead, no one knows anything about it but just you and me."

"Oh, my Godfrey," she said. "When do we get started?"

"Right now. Let's just throw a few things together. Pack some food, just enough to get us to the nearest town with a stage. We'll take the stage to the nearest railroad station, and we'll be on our way. We'll take along a bottle of whiskey or two. A change or two of clothes. Just enough to get us on the way. Then we'll buy everything new. You ready, Sugar Tits?"

She threw her arms around his neck and kissed him hard on the mouth. "Mac," she said.

"What?"

"You don't need to call me by that name no more. My real name is Beverly Butts."

"Well," Mac said, "Beverly is a right pretty name, and we'll be changing that other one right away."

Slocum, Bradley, Morales and Julia rode up to the big ranch house on the Hodges place. Julia was not in a good mood. Slocum dismounted and tied his Appaloosa to the rail in front of the ranch house. He turned to help Julia down from her horse as Eli Basset came walking up.

"Howdy, Slocum," Basset said. He removed his hat. "Miz Hodges."

"Howdy, Eli," said Slocum. "Where's the boss?"

"He got tired of waiting for you to get back," Basset said. "Took some boys and rode off a-looking for you. Left me in charge here temporary."

"I'll be damned," Slocum said. "Hell, I guess I can't blame him. It did take a while."

Julia was considerably relieved to find out that Hodges was not at home. She flounced up the stairs to the porch and jerked open the front door. Then she went inside without a word to anyone. Slocum turned to his remaining two partners. "You might just as well come on down, boys," he said. "We'll have to wait around here till Hodges gets back if we want our money."

Bradley and Morales dismounted. "You want me to take care of the horses, Slocum?" Bradley asked.

"Sure," Slocum said. "Then come on back over here. We'll have something ready to eat."

Sheriff Hardy and his posse were heading into Bentley when they saw the buggy coming toward them. They got in its way on purpose, and it came to a halt. Mac and Beverly were both nervous at the sight of the sheriff, but Mac especially stayed cool on the outside. "Howdy, Sheriff," he said. "You look like you're headed into Bentley."

"That's right," said Hardy. "We're looking for Olaf Johnson."

"Olaf never came back," Mac said. "There ain't no business left in Bentley, so Beverly and me decided to clear out while we can. We're going to find a bigger town where we can make a decent living."

"That fellow Maxie still setting there with his leg propped up?"

"No. Maxie decided he was going out to look for Olaf, so he took off with that leg sticking straight out to one side of his horse. When we left out, there wasn't a soul in Bentley."

Hardy took off his hat and wiped his brow with a sleeve. "I'll be damned," he said. "Everything's a dead end. I guess we'll go in and look the place over anyhow. Well, good luck to you folks."

"Any place we land will be livelier than Bentley," said Mac. The posse rode around the buggy and headed on into the town, and Mac whipped up the buggy. "I hope we can get far enough away from here before they discover that fresh grave," he said.

Hardy led his posse right up to the front of the saloon. They all dismounted and walked inside. Two cowboys were sitting at the bar drinking. There was no one else in sight. "Where is everyone?" Hardy asked.

One of the cowboys shrugged. "Ain't no one here," he said. "We come in for a drink is all. When we found the place empty, we just helped ourself."

"You ain't seen no one?"

"Not a soul."

"All right," said Hardy. "Let's look this whole damn place over. Couple of you boys go upstairs. You two go next door to the store. Look out in the stable. Search the whole damn place."

While the posse scattered, Hardy walked around the saloon. There was nothing to see. He stepped out the back door for a look around. There was a stack of boxes of empty whiskey bottles just outside the door. He did not notice that the ground underneath them was freshly dug. He turned and walked back in. Pretty soon the rest of the posse was back in the saloon.

"Anyone find anything?" Hardy asked.

"There's four horses in the stable," said one man.

"Anyone else?"

"There's nothing, Sheriff. I mean, it looks like it's lived in, but there ain't no one around nowhere."

"Well, shit," said Hardy, and he kicked the nearest chair across the room.

"Sheriff?" said one of the cowboys at the bar.

"What?"

"If you don't mind, what is it you're looking for?"

"We come here looking for old Olaf Johnson. You know him?"

"Sure. Him and his whole crew. They're almost always in here. That's how come we was so surprised when we found the place empty like this. Mac and Sugar Tits is always here too."

"We met them out on the road. They said they was looking for a bigger town and better business. Only thing is, he called her Beverly."

"Beverly?" said the cowhand.

"Beverly," said Hardy.

"Well, I'll be damned," said the drover. "I never thought about it, but I reckon she'd ought to have a regular name just like everyone else."

"Johnson and his crew have been out on the prairie,"

Hardy continued. "All of them got themselves killed except for Johnson and Maxie. We were hoping to find them here."

"Well, you know more than we do," said the cowboy. "The only thing I can suggest is that since there ain't no one around to collect your money, you all have a drink on the house. You look to me like you could sure use it."

"I damn sure can," said one of the posse.

"Hell," said Hardy, "let's all have us a drink. God damn it, we might just get drunk."

"Let's just have us a party," said the cowhand. "You all can call me Tex. This here is my pard, Smiley."

O'Neill and his cowboys had not yet made it to the Hodges ranch when the day drew to an end. It frustrated him, but O'Neill decided that they had to stop for the night. They unsaddled their horses and put them out to graze, built a fire and started a meal and coffee, and laid out their bedrolls. A little later they tied the horses all to a picket line for the night. O'Neill was thinking that Slocum and Julia were likely already back at the ranch. He and his bunch should get there by mid-morning. It would soon be all over. And none too soon for him.

"Boss," said Simp Culley, "we ought to think about stopping for the night."

"We can push on a little farther," said Hodges. "O'Neill is ahead of us. I don't want him reaching the ranch before us."

"Hey," said Culley. "Look up ahead."

"Is that a camp fire?" Hodges asked.

"I'd say so."

"Hold up here, men," said Hodges. "Culley, send someone up there to scout it out."

"I'll go myself," said Culley. "Just wait right here for me."

Hodges and the rest dismounted while Culley rode ahead alone. He rode as near to the site of the fire as he dared. Then he dismounted and worked his way along beside the creek there, creeping and moving as cautiously and as quietly as he could manage. Hiding in bushes and behind a tree trunk, he looked toward the fire. He squinted until he recognized Loren O'Neill. He looked around some more, spotting the picketed horses down by the creek. Then he made his way back to where Hodges and the rest waited for him. He told Hodges the layout.

"Boss," he said, "me and another guy could cut their horses loose and scatter them all over hell. They'd be all night and way into morning gethering them up. Then we could ride a little wide around them and get well ahead of them. Hell, knowing the trouble they'd be in, we might could go on and ride the rest of the way in to the ranch. We'd get there well ahead of them."

"Do it, Simp," said Hodges.

Culley chose a cowhand named Gilmore to ride with him. While they retraced Culley's earlier path, Hodges and the others rode wide of the campsite, heading on toward his ranch. Culley and Gilmore stopped where Culley had stopped before. "Gil," said Culley, "when you hear a commotion, bring the horses up fast. I'll be a-running back this direction. Pick me up, and we'll get the hell out of here."

"I got you, Simp," said Gilmore.

Culley slipped back to where the horses were picketed. It looked to him like most of the cowhands were asleep. There were a couple of them still lingering around the fire drinking coffee. He slipped a knife out of a halter at his belt and cut the line. Then he loosed all the horses. All of a sudden then, he slapped horses on their butts. He yelled and whistled, and he pulled out his six-shooter and fired a few shots into the air. The horses all nickered and stamped and reared. Then they ran. They ran in all directions, and Culley ran too, back toward where Gilmore was waiting, where Gilmore should be riding toward him.

Culley's job did not call for much running on foot, and he was about out of breath when he saw Gilmore. Gilmore was riding hard and leading Culley's mount. He did not slow down. Culley braced himself, and as his horse was about to pass him by, he grabbed the saddle horn and swung himself up into the saddle. As they rode fast after Hodges and the

other hands, they could hear O'Neill and his bunch shouting
and chasing horses. Culley snickered as he rode. He wished
that he could have stayed to watch the sorry bastards climbing out of their bedrolls, pulling on boots and running after
spooked horses in the middle of the night. It would have
been a hell of a good show.

Smiley was on top of the bar dancing and singing an old
Irish tune, while Tex, still on his bar stool, slapped the
counter in rhythm to his partner's antics. The members of
the posse were having as much fun as were the two cowboys,
a couple of them trying to keep up with the song and a couple more dancing out on the floor. They had long since dis-
pensed with the glasses. Every man in the saloon had a
bottle in his hand. All were having the time of their lives.
There was plenty of booze and no one there to take money
from them. It was the party of a lifetime, except there were
no women. Only Sheriff Hardy sulked. He sat with his bottle
at a table in the back of the room, scowling at his posse. He
could not recall a time in his entire life when he had been so
damned frustrated. Nothing was going right. He had gone
out in pursuit of four bank robbers. All four were dead, but
there was no sign of the stolen money. He and his posse had
gotten into two shooting matches. There were dead men all
over the damned prairie, but nothing added up. His only clue
now was Asa Hodges. He had let Hodges get away from him
once with a tall tale. He swore to himself that would not happen again. Smiley fell off the bar and lay still on the floor.
The saloon rang out with laughter. One of the posse men
stumbled and fell and did not get up. Let them have their
fun, Hardy thought. We'll ride out of here in the morning,
hangovers and all. We'll get that Asa Hodges, the son of a
bitch.

Slocum decided that they should watch through the night
just in case. He did not want to be surprised by anyone. He
volunteered to take the first watch; Morales would take the
second and Bradley the third. Slocum posted himself in a

chair on the front porch of the big ranch house. From there he would be able to see anyone who was coming down the lane. He supplied himself with a bottle of whiskey and a glass, but he sipped the whiskey slowly, having no intention of getting himself drunk. He took out a cigar and lighted it. He was surprised at how calm and relaxed he was, even though he still had not figured out just how to deal with Hodges when he returned. All he knew was that he meant to get his money and then to somehow get Julia away from the ranch. If he collected his money, he would have kept his bargain. He would have delivered Julia back to her husband. At that point, all deals would be off. He would feel no qualms about getting her away again. He had made no promise to keep her there after she had been delivered. He was also surprised at how soon his watch was over. Morales came up onto the porch. Slocum took the bottle. He did not trust Morales to just sip a little. He picked up his Winchester and walked off the porch. "Holler at me if you see anyone coming," he said.

"Sure thing, Slocum," said Morales, as he took up the chair Slocum had been sitting in.

Slocum walked on around to the side of the house. He had already laid out his bedroll. He did not want to sleep in the bunkhouse that night. He wanted to be close by if Morales or later Bradley should call. He was about to sit down on the ground to pull off his boots when he heard his name called in a quiet voice. He glanced toward the house. Julia was at a window.

"Everything's all right," he said. "We're keeping watch."

"I want to talk to you," she said.

"What about?"

"Will you come in the house?"

"Morales is sitting on the porch," he said. "It wouldn't look too good if I was to go in the house."

"Come in the back door," she said.

Slocum did not think it was the best idea, but he walked around to the back anyway. Julia met him there holding the door open. He walked in, and she shut the door.

"Come with me," she said. He followed her, still holding his bottle and glass. He had laid his Winchester down on the bedroll outside. "Be careful," she said. "I don't want to light any lamps."

He followed her into a bedroom.

"Sit down," she said.

"What is it you want to talk about?"

"I want to talk about my future," she said. "What did you think?"

For the first time, he really looked at her. She was standing between him and the window wearing a flimsy nightgown. The moonlight beaming through the window silhouetted her shapely form almost as if she had on nothing. He couldn't have kept his eyes off her, even if he had wanted to. He looked her up and down, and he could not find anything wrong with what he saw. She was a beautiful lady.

19

Slocum felt a bit uneasy. Here he was in a bedroom at night with a married woman, and the woman's husband was his boss. It was a situation he did not care to be in ordinarily, but Julia was a damn good-looking woman, and it was not as if he would be the first to take advantage of her unhappy marriage. She had been living with Loren O'Neill for some time now. The other thing, and the biggest thing of all in this situation, was that she did not like her husband. She said that he was abusive, and others said it too. It seemed to be common knowledge. Because of that, Slocum did not like him either. He had no use for a man who would mistreat a woman.

Slocum had spent some time by now with this woman. He had talked with her, and he had looked at her, and he had thought about a situation just like the one he found himself in at this moment. Yes. He had definitely thought about it. Even though it had not been his original intent, he had guards posted outside so he should not be interrupted. It was an almost ideal setup. God damn that Hodges, Slocum thought. If the son of a bitch knew how to treat a woman properly, Slocum would have nothing to debate with himself about. He would just collect his money and ride on about his business.

"You said you wanted to talk," Slocum said.

"Yes. About my future," she said. "Remember?"

"I recollect," he said. "Well, go ahead."

"I want to know what's going to happen to me."

"I'll tell you all I know," Slocum said. "When your— When Hodges comes back, I mean to collect my money from him. Then my job will be done. I'll have kept my word. To tell you the truth, I ain't thought much about what'll happen after that."

"He might kill me," she said. "You don't even care?"

"I never said that. I guess I shouldn't have said that I ain't thought about it. What I meant to say was that I ain't come up with nothing. I just don't rightly know what to do when that time comes. Julia, I don't mean to just ride off and leave you here with a man like that. I just—Well, I just ain't sure exactly what I'll do."

She stepped over close to him and reached her arms around his neck. He responded by encircling her waist with his arms, and they pulled each other close. He leaned forward slightly as she tilted her head back, and their lips met in a soft kiss that grew more and more passionate, until they were each trying to crush the other's mouth, and their lips parted, and their tongues shot out and dueled. At last they broke apart, gasping for breath. Her hands slid down, pulling out his shirttail and working their way up under the shirt.

"You don't have to do this just to get me to help you out," he said. "I promise you I'll figure out something."

"Well," she said, "then let's do it just because we want to. Do you want to?"

"Oh, yes, I do," he said.

Together they walked over to the bed. Julia turned to pull down the covers. Slocum sat in a nearby chair to pull off his boots. Then he stood up and tossed his hat onto the chair. He pulled the shirt off over his head and dropped it on the hat. Next his gunbelt came off and finally his jeans. When he was stark naked, he looked up to discover that Julia had been faster than he was. She was already lying in the center of the bed, her legs laying apart displaying the delights of her crotch. Her body was everything he had imagined it would be. It was more. It was gorgeous and voluptuous and inviting.

Her breasts were full and rounded. Her stomach was flat. Her waist was slim, and below it, her hips widened just enough. Her legs were long and shapely, and they moved around on the bed in anticipation of things to come. Slocum did not keep her waiting. He crawled on top of her, between her legs. His rod was already growing, but when her hands reached down and grasped him by the balls and fondled him there, it grew hard and stiff and ready. She slid one hand up and felt the readiness. "Ooooh," she said, and she guided its head to the wet slit between her thighs. She rubbed it up and down a few times, then plunged the head into her damp and waiting hole. Slocum shoved forward, moving in deep, as she thrust her hips upward to meet him.

"Oh," she said. "Oh. Oh. Oh."

"Ah," he said, and he began to pump slowly in and out, enjoying the feeling of her silky wet flesh.

"Oh," she said. "Fuck me. Fuck me."

He started moving more quickly, humping in and out, and her upward thrusts matched his. He moved faster and faster. Then he stopped suddenly and pulled out. He took hold of one of her lovely legs and raised it up, moving it in front of his body and rolling her over onto her stomach. She quickly scrambled up onto her knees, and Slocum found the slit again and drove himself into it. He pounded into her, slapping himself against her magnificent round buttocks again and again.

"Oh, yes," she said, loving the slapping sound and the feeling of the thrusts. "Oh, yes."

He pounded into her over and over again, faster and faster. Looking down at her back and down her sides, he could see her tits shaking with the action. Then he stopped again and pulled out again. He lay down on his back. Taking her by the waist, he guided her astraddle of his own body. She took hold of his throbbing cock and sat down on it, taking it all the way back into her still hungry pussy. Then she started to rock back and forth on his stomach, her own juices running down and creating a slick surface for her movements. She came again and again and again. At last, exhausted, she fell forward on his chest. She kissed him passionately on the mouth.

"I can't take any more," she said. "You've worn me out."

She slid back, and his tool popped out of her, slapping itself against his belly. She continued backing up until her face was right over it, and then she licked it up and down, at last slurping it into her mouth. She bobbed her head up and down along its length, until at last Slocum felt the pressure building up in his balls, and then he spurted forth into her mouth again and again. When she was certain she had sucked the last drop, she crawled back up to lay with her head on his shoulder. He fondled a tit with his free hand. She reached down and played with his softening cock.

"That was good, Slocum," she said. "Slow to come." She laughed softly at the joke she made. "I'm glad we did it. It might have been the only chance we'll ever have. If things work out right tomorrow, I'll find a way out of here."

"I'll help you," he said.

"And then I'll be on my way back east. We'll not likely ever see one another again."

"I guess it ain't likely," Slocum agreed. "Are you ready to go again?"

Hardy and his posse rode slowly with their heads hanging low. Most were moaning as they rode along. They had not wanted to move when Hardy began rousing them up in the morning, but he had been loud and insistent. One of the men had come walking down the stairs in a woman's dress he had found in one of the upstairs rooms. Hardy had angrily ripped it away. Happily, the man had his own clothes on underneath. Smiley and Tex had both stirred because of all the noise, but they did not get up. Tex did reach for a bottle and take a drink. Hardy caught one of his men doing the same, and he slapped the bottle away from the man's hand. At last he had gotten them all outside and mounted up. They had started the ride toward Hodges's ranch. Maybe they would be all right, or close to it, by the time they reached their destination.

Hardy himself had not had the fun the others had been having, but he had taken in a pretty fair amount of the free whiskey. His head was pounding, but he did not let on. He was thinking that he could sure use a good breakfast and some hot coffee. He kept those thoughts to himself as well. He just hoped that each son of a bitch in his posse was suffering at least as much as he was.

Slocum was sitting on the front porch with a cup of coffee. The sun was just peeking over the horizon. The smells of breakfast cooking for the cowhands were wafting over from the cook shack, but Slocum had already had his. Julia had cooked him a fine breakfast in the big house. Bradley and Morales had managed to get to the head of the line in the cook shack and eat before anyone else. They were finished and Slocum saw them walking toward him. "Morning, boys," he said as they stepped up onto the porch.

"Morning," said Bradley.

"What do we do now?" said Morales.

"Wait," said Slocum.

"How soon you reckon Hodges will show up here?" Bradley asked.

"I don't know," Slocum said.

"You want me to ride out and see if I can see them coming?" Morales asked.

"That ain't a bad idea, Esteban," Slocum said. "When you see any sign of them, ride back here fast and let us know."

"I'll do it."

Morales hustled over to the corral and saddled up a horse. In a few minutes he was riding through the main gate. Slocum and Bradley watched him disappear up the trail heading west. Julia stepped out onto the porch and saw Bradley there with Slocum. "Good morning," she said. "Can I get you a cup of coffee?"

"Yes," Bradley said. "Thank you, ma'am."

She looked at Slocum. "You want some more?"

He handed her the cup. "That'd be real nice," he said. Julia went back inside. A moment later she returned with two steaming cups of coffee. She handed the cups to the two men, then dragged a chair over near Slocum and sat down. Bradley was sitting on the steps. Julia watched Slocum take a tentative sip of the hot liquid.

"I don't suppose you've had any bright ideas yet this morning," she said.

"I've had several," he answered. "None of them seem too damn good though."

"Slocum," she said, "I'm not going to put up with any more of his—"

"When he gets here," Slocum said, interrupting her, "I'll start in talking to him. I mean to be paid. Just let me talk to him first. I figure he'll have to go inside to get the money. You stay out here on the porch. Whatever you do, don't go in the house with him. That's as far as I can go with it right now, but just remember what I said. Let me talk, and don't go in with him."

"All right," she said.

"Slocum?" said Bradley.

"What is it, Bucky?"

"Are you up to something?"

"Nothing for you to worry about. You'll get your money, if I get mine. That's all you need to be concerned with."

"I ain't worried about getting paid," Bradley said. "I trust you. I just want you to know that if you got something else up your sleeve and you need some help, I'm with you."

Slocum smiled. "Thanks, Bucky," he said. "Right now, I ain't sure what I'm going to do, but you just keep your eyes and ears peeled and stay close."

"I damn sure will."

"Who's that?" Julia said. She was looking toward the gate. Slocum and Bradley saw where she was looking and both turned their heads.

"Esteban coming in," said Bradley.

In another minute, Morales was dismounting in front of the porch. "I found a high place," he said. "Hodges is coming with a few hands. He ought to be here in half an hour. But there's another bunch back behind him. A big bunch. I couldn't see them real good, but I'd bet money it's that Big O bunch."

"Oh God," said Julia. "I never thought that Loren would come all the way in here."

"It seems like no one wants to turn you loose," said Slocum. "Well, hell, I guess I can't blame them none."

"What are you going to do?" Julia asked Slocum.

"You just remember what I said while ago," he answered. Then he turned to Bradley. "Bucky," he said, "you run over to the bunkhouse. Tell them what Esteban just told us. Tell them there's liable to be a big fight out here, and the boss'll need them all."

"Okay," said Bradley, getting up on his feet. "I'll tell them."

He turned and ran toward the bunkhouse.

"What about me, Slocum?" said Morales. "What you want me to do?"

"Go put your horse away," Slocum said, "and come back here with your rifle."

Morales mounted his horse and headed for the corral. Slocum's Winchester was leaning against the front wall of the house near the door. He got up and walked over to get the rifle. Then he went back to his chair and sat down again. He took out a cigar and lit it.

"You sure are calm," Julia said accusingly.

"No sense in getting excited."

"You could get killed here in a few minutes."

"That's always the way of it," he said.

Bradley came back, followed by the rest of Hodges's hands. Slocum spotted them around the yard, behind hay bales and an empty wagon, one around each of the front corners of the big house. He kept Bradley on the porch with him. Then Morales came back. Bradley went down off the porch to meet him. They stopped in the middle of the yard and talked in low tones. Then they walked together up to the porch. "I told him what we were talking about earlier," Bradley said to Slocum. "He's with us."

"All right," Slocum said. "You two get one at each end of the porch."

Silence hung heavy in the air for the next several minutes. Then they saw Hodges leading his small band and riding down the trail to turn through the main gate. He led his bunch right up to the porch and dismounted. He stood for a moment looking at Slocum and Julia there on the porch. He looked around some more, at the rest of his men set up for a coming fight.

"Well, Slocum," he said. "I see you brought her back."

"I said I would."

"It took you a time."

"We ran into some snags," Slocum said. "But we're here, and I want to be paid."

Hodges raised a hand and waved it at the cowhands all around the yard. "What's all this?" he asked.

"You may not know it," said Slocum, "but that big bunch of O'Neill riders is coming up right behind you. They'll be along just anytime."

"Are you sure?"

Slocum jerked a thumb toward Morales. "Esteban rode out a ways. He saw you coming, and he saw them coming along after you."

"Damn," said Hodges. "I knew he was headed this way, but I thought the son of a bitch would turn back when he got close to the ranch."

"Not this time," said Slocum.

Hodges turned to face the men who had been riding with him. "All right, boys," he said. "Put your horses away and then get your asses right back here. We might have a big fight on our hands."

The cowboys all rode toward the corral. Hodges walked up on the porch close to Julia. Slocum took note of the ugly sneer on the man's face.

"It's nice to have you back, my dear," Hodges said. Julia did not respond.

"What about my money?" said Slocum.

"Can't it wait till after the fight?"

"One of us might be dead by then. I want to be paid."

"Oh, all right," said Hodges. "Come with me."

Slocum followed Hodges into the house. Hodges moved around behind a big desk and took a key out of his pocket. He sat down and unlocked a drawer. He took out a stack of bills and tossed them onto the desktop. Slocum picked up the pile and thumbed through it. It was all there, all that Hodges had promised him. He stuffed it into his shirt. "Let's get back out there now," he said.

"I'll be along," said Hodges. "Tell my wife to come in here."

"Now, that will wait," said Slocum. "We've got a big bunch of cowhands barreling down on us. I want you out there with us."

Hodges hesitated. He looked hard into Slocum's face, but Slocum did not flinch. He did not move. Hodges sighed and stood up and walked toward the door. Slocum followed him out. The hands who had ridden with Hodges had put away their mounts and were returning to the front of the big house. Hodges had them all line up in front of the big porch with their rifles. He stood on the porch beside Slocum. Julia was standing against the wall a few feet away from the door.

"Hell," said Hodges, "I don't think they'll be here for a while yet. I run off their horses last night. I bet they ain't even caught them all yet."

"Listen," said Slocum.

They stood quiet for a moment, and then they could all hear the sounds of a large force approaching. In another moment, the Big O riders appeared.

20

Sheriff Hardy was at his wit's end. He had been looking for the man that had called himself Evans, but he was fairly certain that it was actually Olaf Johnson. But Johnson seemed to have just disappeared. Vanished from the face of the earth. There was absolutely no sign of the old son of a bitch anywhere, nor of the money that he was supposedly carrying with him. He was beginning to wonder if he should have been so quick to buy the story that Hodges had given him. The more he thought about it, the less likely a tale it seemed to be. Hodges could still have the money. He could have made up that story about Johnson just to throw the sheriff off his own trail.

"Sheriff?" said one of the posse members.

"What?"

"What are we going to do?"

"I been thinking on that," said Hardy. "The last thing we know, ole Hodges had the money. He admitted it. Then he said that damn Evans or Johnson or whoever the hell it was stole it. But all we got is his word on that. We know that he had the money. Right?"

"That's right."

"Let's pay a visit to Hodges's ranch."

Just at that moment, all of the Hodges hands were braced for a big battle. The Big O boys had ridden in and stopped their mounts not too far from the front porch of the big house. Cowhands were lined up in front of the porch holding rifles. Others were scattered around the yard and behind the corners of the house. Slocum, Hodges, Bradley, Morales and Julia were all on the porch. It looked to Slocum as if there could be a bloodbath coming. For what seemed like a long moment, no one said a word. Tension was heavy in the air. At last, Hodges broke the silence.

"O'Neill," he said, his voice loud and strong, "what are you doing on my property?"

"You know damn well what I'm doing," O'Neill answered. "I've come for Julia."

"She's my wife, you son of a bitch."

"Yeah? Well, she don't want to be. You had her kidnapped off of my ranch."

"You're the kidnapper."

"How many men are you two going to get killed to resolve this thing?" Slocum interrupted.

"As many as it takes," Hodges said.

"Well, now," said O'Neill, "I didn't come here aiming to get no one killed."

"Then turn around and get the hell out of here," said Hodges.

"I ain't going to ride off just that easy," O'Neill answered.

"I've got an idea," said Slocum.

All eyes turned toward Slocum. Everyone was suddenly quiet.

"Well," said O'Neill. "Let's hear it."

"Seems to me like this fight is just between the two of you," Slocum said. "Ain't no cause to get anyone else killed, is there? Why don't the two of you just shoot it out between you?"

It seemed to Slocum like a good idea. Hodges was a little old. O'Neill would likely kill him. That would solve half of Slocum's problem—and Julia's. He would only have O'Neill left to deal with. Julia would be free of her bad marriage, and with O'Neill and his crowd on Hodges's ranch, with all of Hodges's hands lined up there ready for a fight, he might be able to back O'Neill off. He glanced at Hodges and saw the nervousness in the old bastard's face.

O'Neill swung down out of his saddle. He put the rifle back in the scabbard and took a few steps toward the porch. "Well, Hodges," he said, "what do you say?"

"How do I know your boys will stay out of it?" said Hodges.

O'Neill turned to look over his shoulder. "Boys," he said, "this is just my fight. If the old son of a bitch kills me, I want you to just turn around and ride out of here. You got that?"

"If that's the way you want it, Boss."

O'Neill faced Hodges again. "You afraid to fight me?" he said. "You going to stand behind all your ranch hands and your hired gunslinger?"

Hodges stepped forward. He walked slowly down the steps and out a little farther, facing O'Neill. "I don't need anyone to help me kill you, you little bastard," he said.

Julia stepped over to Slocum's side and put a hand on his shoulder. He turned his head to glance at her and saw her big eyes looking up at him, anxious and desperate.

"Hang tight," he said.

"Go ahead," said O'Neill to Hodges. "Go for it."

"You go for it," Hodges answered. "I don't need no favors from you."

At that moment, Sheriff Hardy and his posse came storming through the gate. O'Neill heard the commotion and looked over his shoulder. Hodges pulled his six-gun and fired, his bullet hitting O'Neill square in the middle of the chest. O'Neill jerked, looked down at the bloody hole in his chest, staggered back a few steps, looked up at Hodges wide-eyed and fell forward dead.

Hardy and his crew rode up close to the house, and the sheriff dismounted. He walked over and looked at the dead man. He looked up at Hodges, six-gun still in hand.

"What the hell's going on here?" he asked.

"Son of a bitch called me out," Hodges said. "It was a fair fight."

Hardy looked toward O'Neill's cowhands, all still

mounted. Several of them nodded their heads in agreement with what Hodges had said. One said, "That's right, Sheriff. Loren called him out."

"Well then," said Hardy, "I guess there's nothing to be done about it."

"If you don't mind," said one of the Big O riders, "we'll just load the boss up on his horse and ride for home. We got no more business here."

"Hell," said Hardy, "I guess I ain't got no objections. Go on ahead."

Three of the O'Neill hands got down from their horses. One took the reins of O'Neill's horse and led it forward while the other two heaved up the body to drape it across the saddle.

"Wait a minute," said Hardy. "I'm looking for the old son of a bitch that calls himself Olaf Johnson—or sometimes Evans. Have any of you seen hide nor hair of him?"

"Last time we seen him," said one of the riders, "Loren left him sitting in the saddle with his hands tied behind his back and a noose around his neck."

"Huh," said Hardy. "So it was you that done that deed."

He waved a hand dismissing the Big O boys, and said, "Get on out of here."

They all turned to ride away. Everyone stared after them until they were almost out of sight. At last Hardy walked over to Hodges, who still held his six-gun in his hand.

"Hodges," he said, "I can't find no sign of that old wolf hunter. The last thing we know about our stolen bank money, you had it. You told me so."

"That's right, Sheriff, and I told you what happened to it."

"Now that's my problem. I got nothing but your word for that, and I'm wondering whether or not I should believe you. A bundle of money like that would damn near tempt Christ."

"Why, you son of a bitch," said Hodges. "Are you accusing me—"

"I ain't accusing no one," Hardy snapped. "Not just yet. I'm questioning. Right now, I'd like for you to put away that six-shooter."

Hodges hesitated a moment. Then he holstered his gun. "All right," he said. "Question away."

"I'm just thinking about that story you told me," Hardy said. "It sounds pretty damn far-fetched."

"It's the truth," said Hodges. "That old bastard just came along and joined in with us. When you came riding up, he called out that it was O'Neill and his boys. We believed him and started shooting. While we was busy defending ourselves, he stole Simp Culley's horse and rode off on it with the money."

"And how'd you come across the money in the first place?"

"I think I told you that already," said Hodges.

"Tell it again. I recollect you said you took it, but I don't recall you saying just how you come to have it in the first place."

"We come across three men, your bank robbers I expect. They had it."

"How'd you come to find out?" said Hardy. "And how'd you get it from them?"

"Well, I—"

"Did you kill them three men?"

Hodges was getting nervous and angry. "No," he said. "We found them killed. We found the money in the saddlebags on one of their horses."

"You expect me to believe that someone killed them three men and left all that money there for you to come across?"

"That must be how it happened," Hodges said.

"Those dead men didn't have no guns on them," the sheriff said. "I'll tell you what it looks like to me. It looks to me like you caught them somehow. Then you took their guns away from them and murdered them in cold blood. You left them laying there and took the money with you."

"No," said Hodges. "That ain't the way it happened."

"Then when you seen us coming, you ambushed us. You might have killed us all, but you seen that bunch of O'Neill's coming after you, so you took off. Then when we come across you later, you made up that cock-and-bull tale about the old wolfer taking off with the money."

"None of that's true," Hodges said. He turned and looked around until he spotted Culley. "Simp," he called out. "Come over here."

Simp Culley joined his boss there in front of the sheriff.

"Simp," said Hodges, "did you hear us talking?"

"Every word," said Culley.

"Am I telling the truth or not?"

"I ain't never heard no truer words spoke," Culley answered.

"I can't take his word," Hardy said to Hodges. "He's with you."

"Well, what the hell do you want from me?" Hodges shouted.

"First off," said Hardy, "I mean to search this whole damn place."

"I ain't going to let you do that, Sheriff. This is my ranch. My home. My property. I don't mean to allow you or anyone else come onto it and insult me like that."

"I don't see how come it should bother you so much, if you ain't got nothing to hide from me."

Simp Culley was getting nervous. He was loyal to Hodges, up to a point, but he did not like bucking the law. He stepped close to Hodges's side and put a hand on the old man's shoulder. "Boss," he said, "let the sheriff and his posse search the place. They ain't going to find nothing. Just wear themselves out a-looking. Then we'll be rid of them. Hell, Boss, he's just doing a job is all."

Hodges jerked away from Culley and stomped back and forth. Then he turned back to face Hardy. "Go on," he said. "Search all you want. Look everywhere. Turn over all the rocks. Look up every cow's ass for all I care." He stomped up onto the porch and jerked open the door. Without a glance back, he said, "Come on in the house, Julia."

"I'll stay out here," she said.

He turned to face her, furious. He stared at her with hate in his eyes. Then he went inside alone and slammed the door behind him. He strode across the room to a liquor cabinet and poured himself a stiff drink of bourbon. Taking the

drink with him, he walked behind his big desk and sat down.
He took a long drink and put the glass down on the desktop.
He was seething with anger. He thought long and hard. Well,
he would let the god damned sheriff search the place until he
was worn out with the looking. He could not deal with Julia
properly with the lawman around anyway. When Hardy and
his posse were gone, he would take care of her. He opened a
desk drawer and removed a shining leather strap. He dou-
bled it and wrapped it around his right hand. Then he
brought it down on his desktop with a loud smack. He would
deal with Julia all right.

Outside, Hardy assigned each of the posse men a place to
search. The horses the men had been riding had all been put
away. He told someone to find all the saddlebags and search
them. He told another to search the bunkhouse. He then took
two men and told them to follow him into the house. Inside,
they opened every drawer. They pulled the cushions up from
the chairs and the large sofa and searched under them. In short,
they looked everywhere. Hodges was growing more and more
impatient as the morning dragged on. He was anxious to send
Slocum and his two cronies on their way and to get the rest of
his cowhands back to work. Then he could go to work on Julia.

Having found nothing inside the house, Hardy and the
two men with him went back outside. Soon the rest of the
posse had gathered back in the yard. No one had found anything. Hodges came out on the porch.

"Well, Sheriff," he said, "are you satisfied?"

Hardy turned to face him. "I'm satisfied that there ain't
no stolen money on this ranch," he said.

"Then you can mount up and take your blasted posse and
get the hell off of my ranch," Hodges said.

"I'll do that," said Hardy, "but I want you to ride with us
back to town."

"What the hell for?"

"I've got some serious questions regarding the manner of
the death of those bank robbers," Hardy said. "And the manner of your getting your hands on that money."

"I'm not going anywhere with you," said Hodges. "I've

been as patient with you as I'm going to be. It's over. Ride out of here."

"Come with me," said Hardy. "I'll put you under arrest if I have to."

Hodges walked forward and went down the steps. He moved closer to the sheriff. He had just shot it out with Loren O'Neill and won, hadn't he? What was this old used up lawman? Nobody. A has-been, if he'd ever been anything. Hodges thought that he could take the man easily. "You'll have to take me," he said.

"Give me your gun," said Hardy.

"Take it," said Hodges.

On the porch, Julia moved close to Slocum. She looked up at him.

"Take it easy," he said. "Let's see what happens."

Hodges jerked his six-gun out of its holster, but as he was about to bring it into play, he snagged the front sight on the edge of the holster. It slowed him down just for an instant. Hardy's revolver was out and cocked and pointed at Hodges's chest. Hodges had a panicked thought run through his mind as he brought his gun up. He thought, I could give up. He thought it, but he didn't say anything. He kept bringing the gun into play. Hardy squeezed his trigger, and his bullet went high. It caught Asa Hodges in the throat. Blood spurted wildly. Hodges staggered. His knees wobbled. His fingers went numb, and he dropped his revolver. His head bobbed from side to side as his eyes went glassy. Then he fell back and landed hard in the dirt. His eyes stared upward, seeing nothing. Blood continued spurting from the ghastly wound.

Sheriff Hardy had taken Simp Culley with him when he left the ranch. Culley had given him no trouble, as the sheriff had told him that all he wanted from him was an official statement. Culley figured that it would be easy enough to lay everything off on Hodges. The posse was gone. Slocum pulled the twenty thousand out of his shirt and called Bradley and Morales over to him. He counted out five thousand each for the two men and handed it to them.

"Holy shit," said Morales. "I never looked for this much."

"Me neither," Bradley said. "Thanks, Slocum."

"You earned it," Slocum said. "Both of you." He turned toward Julia. "When you're ready," he said, "we can start in hunting you up a train back to Pennsylvania."

"I been thinking," Julia said.

"Oh?"

"With Asa dead, I own this place. Don't I? I am his widow."

"I'd say so," Slocum said.

"You know," Julia said, "the West is looking better to me all the time. I think I'll just stay here."

"You mean that?" said Slocum.

"Why don't you stick around?" she said.

"Well, I don't hardly need a job right now," Slocum said, eyeballing the wad of bills in his hand.

"You won't have to work," she said. She reached up, putting her arms around his neck, and pulled his face down to hers for a kiss.

"Ooo la la," said Morales. "Bucky, you watching that?"

"I see it," said Bradley.

Slocum broke loose from Julia, but he stayed close to her, still looking down into her face.

"I might could stick around for a while," he said.

"Hey, new Boss," said Morales. "Can I stick too?"

"Me too?" said Bradley.

Julia looked toward them, smiling, and said, "Sure."

"Why not?" said Slocum.

Some miles north a buggy turned into a way station along a lonesome road. A man came out the door of the house and watched as a man and a woman climbed down out of the buggy. "Howdy, folks," he said.

Mac, the bartender, looked at him and smiled. "Howdy, mister. Does a stagecoach come by here?"

"Be one here in a couple of hours," the man said.

"Going which way?"

"It'll be headed north."

"To a place where we can catch a train?"

"It'll be a two-day ride, but it'll get you there."

Mac turned to face Beverly. She smiled up at him. "It'll be a two-day ride to the railroad station," he said. "Then a train ride to San Francisco."

"I can hardly wait," Beverly said.

Watch for

SLOCUM AND THE BIG PAYBACK

326th novel in the exciting SLOCUM series
from Jove

Coming in April!

JAKE LOGAN
TODAY'S HOTTEST ACTION WESTERN!